Maddie & Theo's Adventures: Kakarooni Zoo

*Two children, one kidnapper,
and a dream world.
Can they catch him and make it
back to reality?*

LN SHEFFIELD

Author Academy Elite

This is a work of fiction. All of the characters, organisations, and events portrayed in this novel are either products of the author's imagination or are used fictitiously.

Printed in the United States of America
Published by Author Academy Elite PO Box 43, Powell, OH 43035
www.AuthorAcademyElite.com

Identifiers: LCCN: 2020912934
ISBN: 978-1-64746-382-3 (paperback)
ISBN: 978-1-64746-383-0 (hardback)
ISBN: 978-1-64746-384-7 (ebook)
Available in paperback, hardback, e-book, and audiobook

Book design by Jetlaunch. Cover design by Debbie O'Byrne.

For Maddie Reeves—my inspiration for the main character. Maddie is an amazing young lady who knows wholeheartedly how to have fun. She is a fantastic little character, and I am hoping she doesn't lose this too quickly. I am pleased to say she is one of my favourite teachers in life, and I am happy to call her my best friend. Keep smiling and having fun, Maddie.

To)

Finlay,

Always believe in magic
Always have fun
Life is a playground

loads of love,
Lu xxx

CONTENTS

PROLOGUE

Maddie was always on the lookout for mischief.

Last Tuesday, she roamed the back garden. She loved that place—there was always something new to look at or to smell. At the minute the yellow roses were her favourite. The smell reminded her of candy floss, and the petals were soft and velvety. She always felt a warm, fuzzy glow inside of her when she touched them.

It was a spring afternoon. The sun shone bright as a gold button in the blue sky, white clouds were dotted about, and a light breeze made the trees do a little dance.

Maddie had blonde hair and a grin that made her blue eyes sparkle. She was an outgoing, inquisitive eight-year-old who loved to have fun.

That afternoon she discovered something she had never noticed before. Tucked away in the corner of the garden that her Aunt Martha kept so neat and tidy was an old, rusty shed.

Behind it, she found a broken fence with a missing panel.

Maddie wondered what might be on the other side. She looked from left to right to see if anyone was watching. Then she poked her head through. Without a second thought, she squeezed her whole body through the gap and popped out on the other side.

Her eyes opened wide with astonishment. She felt butterflies in her tummy. She found an old, deserted railway station right here at the back of her garden. How could she not have known it was there?

Maddie thought of all the adventures she could have here. She let out a scream of joy and joined the trees in their dance.

Now, where should I begin? she thought to herself.

CHAPTER 1

The Deserted Railway

Theo's brother bored him, going on and on about his stupid girlfriend. Girls were stupid and smelt funny in Theo's opinion. He was determined never to be all soppy over one like Tim was. At nine years old he was a bit of a geek, and he didn't like his round, chubby face, his messy haircut, or his annoyingly long eyelashes.

Tim was at the puberty stage. He had just turned thirteen, and a strong bout of acne spread across his face.

At school, the kids called him pizza boy. Theo felt a little sorry for him, but he knew Tim could look after himself.

The two brothers were out walking. Theo had promised their mother he would pick up a pint of milk on his way home.

"Right, bro, be good. Don't forget the milk for mum, will ya? I'm off to see my lovely girl now. Tell mum I'm playing footie in the park with the lads, will ya?"

"Yes, I'll tell her. But Tim—"

"Make sure you cover for me. Good lad. Have fun, and I'll see you later on." Tim was cocky and confident. He ruffled Theo's hair and left him standing there. He whistled as he waltzed off.

Theo never took any notice of his brother talking to him like this—he was used to Tim cutting him off. He never got a chance to speak around him.

"I hope you have fun with Mel," Theo shouted after him, but Tim was already gone. Theo turned and headed towards the shop.

As he turned the corner, something caught his eye. Across the road on the other side of the tree-lined street, Theo spotted a large, empty space. He had never noticed it before. He often came down this street to the shop, so he wondered why he had never seen it. It was as though there had been something there, and now it was gone.

Maybe a building was knocked down recently, Theo thought to himself.

Out of the corner of his eye, he saw a large yellow poppy. He loved poppies. He loved how they opened up until they were tired and had enough of the day, then closed themselves up and went to sleep.

Although he was quite shy and unsure of himself, today his interest was piqued, so he crossed the street to find out more.

As he got closer to the empty space, he saw a girl admiring the large yellow poppy. He felt a sudden jolt of nervousness and decided he would go off home. Right as he turned to leave, she shouted to him.

"Hey, who are you?" she asked.

Theo felt his cheeks flush a bright red. *Oh no, what was he to do now?* The girl marched towards him. He tried to think fast but felt that familiar panic rise in his throat. His heart beat as loud as a drum in his chest.

"Hi, I'm Theo," he answered. His voice was quiet. He stood still with his head down. "I can't really stay. I have to be heading home now."

"You can't go! I would love a friend to help me look around. I have just found this place, and I think it is an old railway station. There will be loads of exciting things we can get up to here. Please stay," she begged as she bounced towards him and reached out to squeeze his arm. "I'm Maddie, by the way."

He jumped from her grasp, but he looked her up and down. He thought she was pretty. He felt the urge to give her a hug but would never dare do such a thing. He worried a lot about what people thought of him. His gaze fell to the floor where he noticed a shiny penny hidden under a weed. He tucked his hands into his pockets. He was too shy to look at her for very long, and he didn't understand why he hadn't run away yet. This wasn't normal for him. He loved her cheeky smile, and he felt drawn to her confidence.

"I can't. I have to fetch milk for my mum," he answered, cautiously moving away a little more.

She stared at him, which made him even more uncomfortable. He wasn't used to girls. Maddie moved towards him and grabbed his hand. She pulled him over to the place where the poppy grew.

"Isn't it beautiful?" she asked him. It grew in a small crack in the concrete. They didn't stay with it too long, though, as Maddie seemed desperate to get exploring. He soon realised she wasn't going to let him get away.

"Come on, this way."

She still gripped his hand as they walked towards what looked like an old wooden shack. Maddie took the lead. As they approached the shack, they realised the door was around the other side, out of view of the street. Theo noticed a padlock on the handles. It was very old, the hinges were rusted, and there was a huge bolt at the top. It was clear there was no getting inside. Wooden boards covered up the windows, too. It smelt damp in the air and felt cold and unloved.

Overhead, the birds sang in the blue spring sky, perched upon a telephone wire. For a brief moment they distracted Maddie, but she continued to search for a way inside.

"Wow, look at that, Maddie." Theo's face lit up with excitement as he pointed across the track. He lost himself for a moment, his shy, nervous persona forgotten. Maddie was right. It was clearly an old railway station they had stumbled across. They stood on the platform. Maddie shifted her attention from the task at hand as she followed Theo's gaze.

On the other side of the deserted railway track, they saw an old, multi-coloured train carriage with no door. Someone had been there and covered it with graffiti art. Maddie ran to the edge of the railway track with widened eyes. Theo hung back. He watched her body bounce with an excited energy.

"Come on, Theo, don't be scared. It's deserted here. We will be safe to cross the track. Trust me." Maddie's kind eyes eased his nerves as he joined her at the edge of the track.

Theo followed Maddie as she lowered herself from the platform onto the track. It wasn't a long way down in reality, not like how they made it look in films. It smelt funny though, sort of damp and rusty. The air was very still, and a lot of weeds and grass had grown over the track, making it soft and padded underfoot. A large willow tree loomed overhead. Theo noticed a lot of rubbish dumped along the track. Maddie held out her hand to Theo as they scrambled across to the other side.

Once they had heaved themselves up onto the other side of the platform, they sat on the edge for a moment to take in the atmosphere. It was peaceful. Only the birds singing overhead made any sound, and a light breeze caused the trees to dance and the leaves to swoosh about.

Disturbing the peace, Maddie frowned and jumped up. "What is it?" Theo asked. She walked over to the bench just behind them. On it was a blue suitcase. She opened it without caution and shouted.

"Come and look, Theo. It's full of clothes." Maddie began pulling articles of clothing out of the case and flinging them onto the bench and the floor. A layer of dust lifted from the clothes and made her sneeze.

Theo dragged himself up and wandered over to see what all the fuss was about.

"What are you looking for?" Theo asked her. He thought she had gone mad, throwing the clothes everywhere without a care in the world. "I thought we were going to look at the old train carriage."

"I'm not sure, but I just have this feeling I need to find something. Why would there be an old suitcase here just lying about for no reason? There must be something in here that is important." Theo didn't understand what she meant. He felt uneasy. He continued to stare at her as she tore the suitcase apart.

"Maybe we should go home. We could get ourselves into trouble, Maddie. This stuff might belong to someone. I'm a little scared." Theo's voice shook as he spoke, and his eyes darted about. He shivered. The air around them had a chill to it.

Maddie stopped her frantic search and turned to face him. Before he knew what was happening, she hugged him tight.

"Please, Theo, trust me and don't leave. We are going on some amazing adventures—I know it. Come on, help me look through the clothes. There is no one here. We are safe."

Theo relaxed a little. "Okay, I'll stay."

He then helped Maddie empty all the clothes onto the bench.

"We should check the inside. What's it called again?" he asked, pointing to the material that lined the case.

"Umm, I don't know. But yeah, good idea," Maddie said, cocking her head to one side.

"I've seen them do it in films." Theo grinned. He was a quick-thinking little lad, good at solving things.

Maddie rummaged around with both her hands in the lining. As he watched, he could tell by the look on her face that she had found something.

"What is it? What have you found in there?" he asked her. He was dying to know.

She pulled her hand out. Her fist was scrunched into a tight ball. "It's a key. And look, there is a note attached to it." She unfolded her hand so he could see it too.

For a moment, they both stood in silence, neither of them knowing quite what to do or what it all meant. A quiet rustling sound came from the track. A rat was rummaging away in some leftover food, seeking his next meal. He scurried away after his eyes met Theo's for a split second. This shocked them both out of their silence, and Theo reached over and grabbed the key from Maddie.

"Let me see it properly," he said. The key felt cold in his palm. It looked ordinary enough. He uncrumpled the note and screwed his face up with confusion. There were three sentences written using symbols. It was written in code. It seemed to be some sort of clue, but it didn't make any sense. However, Theo loved a good puzzle to solve. He liked to get his brain working. Theo kept a secret diary under his mattress, and he wrote in there using symbol codes, so he was sure it wouldn't take him long to figure out what it said. He also relied on Maddie to help.

"What does it say?" Maddie asked him as she peered over the top of the note.

They pushed all the clothes onto the floor and sat down on the bench together to look at the note and see if they could crack the code. Maddie's blank expression said it all.

"It just looks like a load of rubbish. I don't have a clue about this sort of stuff. Are you clever with things like this?" Maddie asked him.

"Well, I do like to try and solve puzzles and things. I also do write using codes sometimes, so I will have a go at it. I can't promise anything though," he replied, feeling his embarrassment in his cheeks.

"I will leave you to have a look at it," she said as she began to fold up all the clothes and pop them back into the suitcase. She didn't like a mess.

The railway station had a peculiar smell to it, especially under the cover where they sat on the bench next to the old, damp wall. Nearby was the toilet block, and even though it was deserted, it had never been knocked down. It reeked of sewage and disturbed Theo's nose.

Maddie decided to go off and investigate for a short while, leaving Theo deep in thought and puzzle-solving mode.

After a few minutes, Theo began to see the pattern of the code. It was very similar to what he used for his diary writing. He didn't want to admit to Maddie he had a diary. He thought she would think he was a wimp. Lifting his head up from the note, he saw her in the distance. He had watched her walk over and poke around at the signal box, and now she was moving back to him. He felt pleased with himself for making sense of the coding—his brother had taught him well. He hoped Maddie would be impressed.

"Any luck, Theo?" Maddie asked, bouncing back down onto the bench beside him.

She's so full of life, he thought.

He smiled at her, stretched out the paper, and said, "Look, I've worked out the first two sentences. I only have to decode the last bit." She leant over and gave him a cuddle. She wasn't shy, and he was getting used to it.

"Yippee, you are the best! I knew you would do it. Come on, then. What does it mean? I'm so excited."

"Well," he began, "it says, 'Maddie and Theo, use this key to unlock the treasure chest. This will reveal your next clue.' And I think the last sentence reads, 'You must search the railway station for the chest.'"

"How do they know our names, Theo? Oh, wow, this is like a magical treasure hunt. I feel like I'm on a TV show or in a film. This is so exciting, isn't it?" Maddie exclaimed, jumping up from the bench and doing a little crazy dance. "Come on, let's go. I think I know where the chest might be."

She soon forgot all about the train carriage again and was dragging Theo by the hand, leading him towards the signal box. He was happy to let her take the lead. He felt a little excited himself about all of this, although he couldn't understand how someone had planted these notes and keys and treasure chests. He liked things to be explained and logical, but nothing that had happened had any explanation.

They walked up to the end of the concrete toilet block. Next to this, they found a small cafeteria area. A sign reading "Station Buffet" hung off the wall, and a few of the letters were missing. The tables and chairs were all still inside, stacked up. The room was dark and dingy. Maddie cupped her hands around her eyes and leaned her face against the glass.

"Look, Theo," she said as she peered into the one window that wasn't boarded up. He copied her and saw a used coffee machine on the counter. A coffee cup was left on the side, green with mould from the stale, half-finished coffee. It looked as if someone had just left mid-shift, and the place had since been abandoned and closed down.

"Yuck! It's all dirty," Theo said.

"Yeah, it's horrible, isn't it? Although the thought of some cake right now sounds nice. I am a bit hungry. Come on, let's go. I want to find this chest."

She pulled Theo away from the window, and they continued past the cafe. There was still no one else about, and the thought crossed Theo's mind whether anyone even knew this deserted railway was here. *Does it even exist?* he wondered, his thoughts suddenly taking on a mind of their own. *Of course it exists*, he thought, ignoring his previous crazy thought. They were here experiencing it. They came to the end of all the buildings, and he remembered the train carriage. That was the reason they had crossed the railway in the first place—to investigate. The blue suitcase had sidetracked their attention.

"Maddie, let's not forget the train carriage. When we have found this chest, I want to go and look at it."

"Yes, of course, me too. Come on, we are nearly at the tall hut." She grinned with wild, hungry eyes.

A few yards in front of them, Theo saw the tall hut Maddie talked about. It was an old signal box. It looked super cool.

"Oooh, this looks cool," Maddie said. Theo could tell she didn't know what it was. It was shaped like a square box with a pointed roof, windows all around the outside, and a set of steps leading up to the door. The walls were painted green and cream.

"Do you think it will be locked, Theo?" she asked. They both stood still and stared up at the building.

A metal gate wrapped around the hut and a sign hung from the front that read, "Public must NOT pass this point." A green lamppost stood on the left-hand side, situated on the unkept lawn. Outside of the gated area was a tall post with signals like traffic lights right next to the edge of the track.

She didn't wait for him to answer her. Ignoring the sign, she pushed the gate open and climbed the steps.

"Oh, wait for me." Theo was shocked that she had gone without a second thought, but he didn't want to miss out, so he followed.

The stairway was old, rusted, and unsafe. Maddie's little plimsoll shoes occasionally slipped on the steps.

They reached the top and tried the door. It was locked.

"Let's go around this way," Maddie said, pointing to the back of the building. There was a small platform around the edge, so they walked round to the back, thinking about where the chest could be. After turning the corner, they discovered a small chest set against the railing, hidden from view. It wasn't much bigger than a jewellery box, but Maddie had a keen eye for spotting things and noticed it straight away.

"Theo, where is the key?" she asked him. He reached into his pocket where he had tucked it away and passed it to her. They both took in a deep breath. Theo closed his eyes as she inserted the key and twisted.

As it clicked, Theo opened his eyes and released his breath.

"It worked. Look at this," she said, pointing inside. There was a small, multi-coloured figurine of an old train carriage. In fact, it was an exact copy of the carriage at the other end of the station.

There was no note this time, only the model train. The pair of them looked at each other in wonder.

"What does all of this mean?" Theo asked.

The sky had begun to cloud over a little more as the afternoon moved on. The birds still sang, and the wind had picked up a jot. Maddie buttoned up her cardigan as a shiver ran through her. There was a quietness in the air, reflecting the desertedness of the railway. They climbed down the steps. Theo clutched the chest in both his hands.

"Come on, Theo. Let's go see the train carriage," Maddie announced once they reached the ground. Theo nodded his agreement as they marched off in the direction they had come from. They were both at a loss to understand what was going on with the chest and the note, but Theo thought the old train carriage might hold more answers.

The carriage was located further up on a side track, abandoned, like most of the things around this railway seemed to be. They left the signal box and headed for the carriage, passing the bench. Theo noticed it first: the bench was empty. He stopped in his tracks.

"Where has the suitcase gone?" Theo asked with a slight glint of fear in his eyes. They hadn't seen or heard anyone else around. He was sure they were the only ones there, but it wouldn't have taken more than a split second for someone to pinch the case while they had been busy climbing and exploring the signal box.

"How strange. I don't know. I'm sure we are the only ones here," Maddie replied, looking around.

Theo felt an air of nervousness about her. She took his hand in a reassuring grip and led him towards the carriage.

• • •

It wasn't very big, only one abandoned coach. Theo wasn't too excited by it, although he did love trains. It looked messy to him. Spray-painted on one side in huge black-and-white block lettering, it read, "Mice." He wondered what it meant and thought it would be better if it said "rats" since they had seen a couple of them around here. It was coloured all over in orange with lots of smiley faces and other random words and signatures. There was also a huge skull and crossbones on the left-hand side and abstract art on the right-hand side.

"Oooh, I love it. Artwork is so cool." Maddie beamed.

For a moment, they walked around the coach, checking it out from the outside. There were a few small windows on each side. Some had glass panels, and some were simply empty holes. The doorway was open, so they could waltz in if they pleased. It looked dark and murky on first glance. Theo felt scared and hung back. But Maddie (being the brave one) turned to him gently and said, "Come on, Theo. It will be alright. There is nothing to be scared of. Let's go inside and see what it's like. It looks exciting."

Theo felt the excitement ooze from her, and his fear dropped a little.

The first thing they noticed inside was the blue suitcase balanced across the front two seats. It was closed and locked. Maddie looked at Theo and back at the suitcase.

"What's that doing in here?" she asked as he latched onto her arm for support. He felt a little unsteady on his feet, and he was scared about the strange things that seemed to be happening to them.

"I don't know. It's all a bit weird, isn't it?" he replied, shaking.

Inside the carriage, all the seats were still in place, but they were all ripped up, and some had graffiti on them too. It was pretty dark. Not much light was able to get in through the tiny glass windows. But it was all intact—nothing missing, merely old and deserted. Again, the familiar smell of dampness filled their nostrils.

"Yeah, it is. I wonder what it is all about. Shall we reopen the suitcase?" she asked him as she sat down on a seat near the front of the carriage. Theo sat next to her. He was still carrying the treasure chest with the model train inside.

"I don't know. I'm scared. What if someone is watching us?" Theo asked.

"Shall we open the chest again, then?" she asked. Theo nodded.

As Theo opened the chest, sparks danced under the lid, and the model train came to life and played a song. It shook so violently that Theo couldn't hold onto the chest. His hands trembled so much that he dropped it onto the floor. The music was getting louder, and the model train was getting bigger, as if it was trying to break out of the chest and grow to the same size as the real carriage. The walls around Maddie and Theo shook vigorously. They stared at each other, eyes wide with fear and astonishment. Theo let out a loud scream while Maddie tried to keep a calm head about her. In the next moment, everything went pitch black.

CHAPTER 2

Kakaroonis, a Cold Library, and Quests Revealed

Maddie felt herself being shaken. As she came round, she opened her eyes, stretched, and jumped up. Theo was next to her. He looked drained. They were on a bench in the middle of some kind of zoo.

"Where are we? What is going on, Theo? And what are those things?" she asked, pointing to the cage.

"I don't know where we are. I've only just woken up," Theo replied. He looked dozy.

Her head felt fuzzy as she glanced about. The zoo was bustling with people, and there were some strange creatures in a cage to their right. In a flash, she remembered the train and the railway station, and all that had happened before she blacked out. *Where are we?* she thought. It didn't seem real. It was like a dream.

They woke on a bench beside a small, round pond. It smelt fresh in the air. Maddie heard the cooing of a wood pigeon in the distance. The water was still and quiet but for the faint trickling of the fountain in the middle of the pond. The surrounding area was very green and crisp. The cobblestone pathway beneath their feet looked shiny and new as if it had just been polished. It was a sheltered area with plenty of silver birch and willow trees casting beautiful reflections upon the water.

Maddie decided to go for a little stroll and see what this place was all about, and Theo joined her. She could smell the faint aroma of barbecue food wafting through the air, teasing her nostrils. She suddenly realised she was very hungry.

• • •

Maddie and Theo talked as they wandered through the park. They both remembered the recent events at the railway station and wondered how they ended up in this strange zoo. They both remembered the same thing happening. Maddie voiced her opinion on it all.

"I think we have been abducted by aliens, Theo, and sent here to rescue a princess. There is a strange force sending us around to other worlds." She giggled. She had a wild imagination.

Before Theo even had time to answer, a very odd-looking owl snuck out from behind a small bush. He had patches of fur and a half-shaved head with a pink streak of hair like a Mohican. Theo eyed him up and down in a suspicious manner while Maddie bent down to stroke the little fella. She thought he was super cute. He spoke with a Jamaican accent.

"Hey, kids! I am a Jamaican owl, you can call me Mr J. I can't stay for long, but I am here to tell you about a quest. You are not here by mistake, but I need to go to Head Office to find out more—"

"What quest? What do you mean?" Maddie butted in.

"I will be back soon," Mr J continued. "While I am gone, go to the Cold Library and have a little wander about the zoo to get familiar with the kakaroonis. Follow the map." He pointed to a large map of the zoo right in front of them.

"But, Mr J, what are you on about?" Maddie asked as she lowered herself to his height.

"All will be revealed. I must go for now—there is work to be done. But have fun. I will catch you later." And with that he was gone, leaving behind a puff of pink-coloured smoke in his absence.

Maddie and Theo stole a long, curious glance at each other, wondering what that was all about and who this strange little creature was. Maddie loved him and wanted to tuck him into her pocket and keep him forever. Theo was anxious and fidgety. Maddie took his small hands in hers, stared into his eyes, and said, "Come on, Theo. Let's have an adventure. Let's do what Mr J says. It will be fun. I think there will be lots of great things to see around this place. Mr J said he will see us later, so come on. I want to go see what these kakaroonis are."

Maddie felt the muscles in his hands relax. The frown dropped from his face as a smile replaced it.

"Do you have magical powers? I feel safe with you, and I know worrying is crazy. I just can't help myself. My mother will be drinking black tea by now," he explained.

Maddie flicked her long blonde hair over her shoulder. It annoyed her, blowing into her face from the light, gentle breeze. That familiar hunger pang from earlier returned. It felt stronger, and she felt a little faint. She wasn't surprised as time was going so fast. She was shocked to find it was dinner time.

"I'm hungry. Shall we stop and get something? Look, there is a burger van on the way," she said, pointing to the map.

Once they reached the van, they ordered some chips and a soft drink each. She figured this was where that delicious barbecue smell came from. Theo found the milk money buried deep in his pocket.

They found a table and sat down to wait for their food.

"How long have you lived in Ainsley, and where do you go to school?" Maddie asked him. She wanted to know everything about him.

"I haven't lived here very long. We moved here about four months ago. I go to Saint Christopher's. Where do you go?"

Maddie took a long slurp of her coke, not realising how thirsty she had been. "I go to St Anne's," she said proudly.

The chips arrived, and Maddie added a large amount of salt and vinegar to hers. Theo tucked his chair in closer to the table and removed his cap as they began to eat. He squeezed the mayonnaise tube all over his side of the chips.

"I love mayonnaise," he smirked.

"I like most things but not mayonnaise. It's so creamy," Maddie said. She stuck her tongue out and doubled over. Theo laughed at her.

Once they were both full, they continued on the same path around the zoo, heading to the Cold Library. There were still plenty of people about even though time was ticking on and the zoo was due to close at dusk. They came across a sign which read, "Cold Library."

"Here we are, Theo. This way."

Maddie took his hand and pulled him past the sign. They came to a large brick building. Theo got the door for Maddie, and as they slipped inside, they joined a long queue.

Maddie tapped the tall man in front of them on his shoulder.

"What are we queuing for, mister?" she asked politely. He turned, bent down, and smiled.

"We are queuing for the special kakarooni food, of course."

"Oh, how cool! I can't wait to see the food. What is it like? And those strange things out there in the cages, are they called kakaroonis, then, mister?" she asked.

"Yes, of course. What else would they be? This is the Cold Library where the kakaroonis have their feeding time. It was originally used only as a library. You will notice all the books in the main room." He pointed to the door which led to the main room.

"When all the kakaroonis were rescued and brought here, this area was the biggest space, and it seemed a great idea to get them all together and make feeding time fun," he continued.

"How many times are they fed in a day?" Maddie asked him.

"Twice—lunchtime at one o'clock and evening time at five-thirty. Wait till you see the food. If you ask nicely, I think the lady behind the counter will give you an information leaflet on the whole zoo and the kakaroonis background. They are magical creatures, worth a fortune!"

"But mister, I have never heard of them before. Is this a real world we are in, or are we dreaming? I have no money to buy any food. We landed here somehow through the train carriage."

Maddie explained the series of events leading them here, forgetting to pause for breath in all her excitement. He looked at her, a little bewildered. She liked him.

"Of course you did, sweetheart. It is all real and yet all made up!" he said, grabbing his wife's handbag and pulling out a rather large pink purse. He slipped a fiver out and handed it to Maddie.

"Treat yourself to some kakarooni food. If you ever find out if this world is real or not, find me and let me know." He winked at her. His eyes were like marbles. It was his turn at the counter. Then he was gone in a flash.

• • •

The room inside the Cold Library was set out with chairs for the adults and bales of hay for the children. Maddie and Theo sat on bales.

Maddie had picked up a leaflet all about the kakaroonis and the zoo. She started to read a few of the highlights to Theo as they waited for the creatures to come in for their feed. She paused to open the bag of food.

"Oh, Theo, look. It's all sparkly and shaped like hearts and stars. And it smells yummy. Look how colourful it is, too, not like the boring dog biscuits we get in the real world." Theo leant across and poked his nose into the bag.

"Oh, yeah. It smells nice," he commented, then sat back in his seat as she continued to read.

"They originate from Ul . . . aan . . . baatar—I can't say that very well. The capital of Mongolia, the world's coldest capital city. The zoo is kept at cold temperatures wherever possible. The kakarooni is an awesome creature, to say the least, consisting of five legs. The fifth leg is located in the middle of their belly, and to help them keep warm, they wear a sock and trainer on the foot of that leg all the time." She paused for breath.

"Kakaroonis are only ever male. They are truly beautiful creatures, multi-coloured like a rainbow. They have cute faces with three huge multi-coloured puppy dog eyes. Their diet consists of the sparkly, colourful star- and heart-shaped biscuits. This food comes from the only place it can be grown—the fields in Ul . . . aan . . . baatar. The kakarooni can also talk just like a human. They are such loving creatures and adore children making a fuss of them. In the library area children can feed them and read to them." She placed the booklet down on her lap. "Oh, here they come, Theo."

The feeding commenced, and the kakaroonis filed into the room. They were similar to kangaroos in size and appearance aside from their special features. Maddie leant over to Theo and whispered in his ear.

"Theo, aren't they pretty? They look so soft and furry. I can't believe how big they are. They look like giant kangaroos."

"Yes, they are very strange looking animals," Theo replied, frowning. He was deep in thought.

This was no ordinary feeding exercise, though. As with most things in this zoo, rules and regulations went out of the window. Kakaroonis were big eaters. They were such large creatures, they needed lots to eat to keep their energy levels up. After all, with five legs, the food needed to spread across a lot of body area. And with all the dancing and entertaining they did in the park throughout the day, it soon got used up. Most of them ate three times a day at least, and any extra snacks were always a welcome treat. They always ate breakfast in their cages.

"Yummy, yummy, yummy, kakarooni food in my five-legged tummy!" one of them chanted as they hopped around on one leg. This was another crazy, favourite trick of theirs. The kakaroonis got excited when their food time came around. They started dancing on one leg and singing songs they made up on the spot and swinging the kids around in the air with their tails.

"This is crazy," Theo commented, although he looked mesmerised. Maddie loved it. She loved crazy stuff, so this was right up her street. She wanted to stay here forever and have fun with these gorgeous creatures.

The madness of the Cold Library feeding session soon came to a halt after only fifteen minutes. By then, the kakaroonis and the children were all ready for a nap. So, next on the list was, of course, what libraries are known for—story time. Story time was also great fun in a different, more relaxing way. All the children began reading to the kakaroonis, but it wasn't long before they fell asleep. Maddie and Theo didn't feel very tired at all, so they stepped over the other children and tiptoed out of the Cold Library.

Once they were outside, Maddie noticed a sign indicating a play area directly opposite them.

"Oh, Theo, look. It's a park. Come on, let's go and play," Maddie said.

"Maddie, we shouldn't. Mr J said we need to get to know the kakaroonis."

"It's okay. Mr J isn't even here yet, and we met the kakaroonis. I'm sure we can play for a minute." A glint of mischief shone in Maddie's eyes as Theo slumped his shoulders and followed her.

The park consisted of a couple of swings, a slide, a roundabout, and a few bouncing boards. They came in different shapes and sprung a person around all over the place. Maddie loved these. They were her favourite thing in the park. They were almost as fun as a bouncy castle, but she often felt much dizzier and struggled to stand up straight once she got off them. She loved that feeling.

There were a few kids playing on the swings while their parents sat on the bench. They were busy with their noses in their iPhones.

It felt eerily quiet for a park, considering the zoo was so busy with people today. The squeak of the swings as the children whooshed into the air was all that could be heard. The air here in this zoo was different from how it had been at the railway station. It felt misty.

"Come on, Theo. Let's play," she shouted with joy as she ran towards the play area.

Maddie removed her shoes and socks, grabbed the railings to steady herself, and jumped into the sand. It was cold on her bare feet.

Maddie couldn't wait to get on the wobbly bouncy boards, and she loved the feel of the sand beneath her feet. She ran across to them while Theo headed for the large slide.

Maddie laughed her head off, bouncing and springing all over the place. She felt all giggly and dizzy. As she bounced around, she caught a glimpse of Theo racing down the slide, a huge grin on his face. He was having a blast, his hair flying backwards from the force of the wind. After a few minutes, Maddie decided to join Theo and play on the slide for a bit. The other children were still on the swings.

"Theo, let's see if we can climb up the slide," Maddie shouted to him as she ran across the damp sand. The grains snuck in between her toes.

"I don't think we should. It's naughty, and there are other children that may want to play on it." He lowered his gaze to the ground as he spoke.

"Yeah, you are right, I suppose." Maddie agreed.

They had a few more goes on the large slide and then made their way over to the roundabout. It was a cool roundabout with red metal handlebars, and the base was painted red and yellow.

Maddie decided to show off and hung herself upside down from the bars.

"Come on, Theo. Stop being scared," she said teasingly.

"No, I might fall. I will spin you and watch."

Maddie laughed as the blood drained to her head. She could see Theo wincing.

They spun each other a couple of times. As the roundabout came to a stop, Maddie looked up and saw the other children making their way over to join them.

"Hi, can we play with you?" the youngest girl asked them. Maddie thought she seemed nervous. There were two girls and two boys. She guessed they were about the same age as Theo and herself.

"Of course you can. It's more fun with more of us," Maddie said.

They all jumped on the roundabout. They laughed and enjoyed the dizziness. They had so much fun. Maddie told them all about how she and Theo got here through the train carriage. As they listened, their eyes widened with enthusiasm and amazement.

After a few more minutes of playing, Maddie and Theo's new friends toddled away to their parents.

The park was then deserted. Theo said he fancied a go on the swings. As they swung in a slow motion, Maddie noticed the sand shifting in strange patterns.

"Theo, look at the sand. It's moving. What do you think it is? A mole or something?" The sand wasn't simply blowing in the breeze. It was moving as if something was in it.

They heard the faint sound of a Jamaican accent. Maddie realised it was Mr J. He sounded agitated. They both slowed down their swings and jumped off, eager to talk to him some more.

"Mr J, you are back. I hope you are going to tell us what is going on. We have been to see the kakaroonis, but now we want to know why we are here, don't we, Theo?" Maddie looked over at him for backup. He nodded his head in agreement, but in true Theo style didn't offer anything further. Maddie knew by now he was happy with her taking the lead.

Mr J waddled over towards the bench. He jumped up and beckoned for them to sit with him. It was still warm from the parents sitting there. Maddie stroked his pink Mohican. He was so cute. Theo grabbed his cap and sat next to Maddie, still eyeing Mr J with suspicion.

"Firstly, what are you doing in the park? You are supposed to be getting to know the kakaroonis! I will let that go for now. However, you must practice doing as you are told. We are going to be working against the clock."

"We did, Mr J," Maddie began explaining, hands on her hips. "We played with them and—"

"Okay, okay," Mr J muttered. "Right, it's time I filled you in on what's happening. There is a company called Imagination World. The team of workers operate from Head Office." He paused for a moment, scratched his cheek with his claw, and shook his feathers. Mr J then continued.

"Head Office is situated just outside of Kakarooni Zoo. The closest place inside the zoo is called Rainbow Slide Park. They are responsible for turning children's dreams into realities. Kakarooni Zoo is a child's dream."

Maddie and Theo looked at each other, taking it all in. So, they were in a dream world. They had been transported there by the events at the railway station.

"This is so cool." Maddie loved the sound of all this. Theo, not so much—he frowned. She knew he struggled to believe in the magic. He had explained to her that he liked logic to understand things.

"The Head Office team is in charge of this zoo," Mr J said. "They oversee everything that goes on here. I'm not quite sure why you have been specifically chosen to come into this imagination world, but I am pretty sure you will be great at helping us solve the quest."

"So, you mean we are here for a quest?" Maddie asked. Her eyes danced with excitement.

Mr J nodded his feathered head.

"Yes! But like I said, I'm not sure of the details yet. I'm certain the team at Head Office will let me know one way or another soon enough. Anyway, I must dash again."

He jumped off the bench.

"Go and check out the kakaroonis in their cages while I attend to some business. Meet me at the exit gate for closing time. Follow the map." And once again the children didn't get a chance to ask anything further or even say goodbye. He was gone, a puff of pink smoke left behind for them to choke on.

Maddie and Theo stayed seated on the bench for a few minutes. At least now things were a little clearer.

"Wow, how cool is this going to be, Theo! I can't wait to hear what the quest will be about. Are you excited? I hope Mr J isn't away too long this time. I want to know more right now." Maddie didn't even give him a chance to answer. She grabbed his hand and dragged him off the bench. "Come on, let's go and see the kakaroonis."

• • •

Visiting the kakaroonis in their cages was a strange experience. Maddie and Theo were allowed to go inside with them, stroke them, and be with them in their home. Inside the cages, they had toys to play with and a television. Once inside the large metal cages, Maddie noticed they had a funny smell to them. It was an earthy smell, like dry soil. However, the ground inside was covered in slab tiles. This helped the area stay quite cool for the kakaroonis.

The kakaroonis were warm and loving creatures, and the children enjoyed the overall experience.

"You are so cute and adorable. I want to take you home," Maddie said to one of the creatures.

"Come and watch the TV with us," the kakarooni suggested.

Maddie and Theo loved this idea. They each cuddled up with a kakarooni. Maddie's kakarooni felt like a giant teddy bear. She loved the safety she felt as he wrapped her in his arms. She looked into his eyes and saw love. She felt it in the way he squeezed her tight. It reminded her of the few times her aunt showed her love, too.

Eventually, the children made their way to the exit to meet Mr J. On their way, Maddie spotted a huge slide in the distance.

"Oooh, look over there, Theo. It's a helter-skelter. I love those." Her grin spread from ear to ear.

Maddie was very tempted to go and play but remembered Mr J's warning about minding their time and doing as they were told.

As they reached the exit, Maddie saw Mr J approaching.

"Hi, kids, been having fun? Right then, I'm back for a while this time," he announced.

"Oh, yippee! We have just been to see the kakaroonis. I am so glad you're back, Mr J. We are so excited to help Head Office. Please tell us more!" Maddie begged him. Her eyes twinkled with delight.

"Well, as the zoo is about to close, we need to do something about freezing the time. I am sure Head Office can help with this. They are very good at what they do," Mr J said.

This idea excited Maddie. She wondered how it was going to happen.

"Head Office will watch on the cameras. They need to make sure everyone else has left the zoo. We need to be the only ones here."

Lots of people were leaving the zoo as it was nearly closing time. The mist lifted a little, and Maddie felt a slight change in temperature. It seemed warmer in the air now.

As they watched everyone leave, Maddie noticed Mr J's expression change—he looked more serious. He lifted his wing and pulled out a cord, then placed it near his ear. She saw what looked like an earpiece attached to the cord. Mr J's face scrunched into a frown. His beak upturned, and his eyes blinked fast. His wings flapped with no control, and his whole little body turned a bright, furious red.

"What's wrong, Mr J?" Theo asked him.

"Well, that was Head Office. There is news of the quest you are needed for. However, it is not good news, kids. Head Office has instructed me to bring you with me so all can be explained."

"I don't understand." Maddie raised her eyebrows. She stared at Mr J, waiting for an answer.

"Things have changed. We have to move right away. There isn't time to say any more. Hop on."

And with that, they were off.

CHAPTER 3

Head Office, Green Men, and Wispy Adninjas

They arrived with a thud. Mr J skidded to a halt after they hit the ground.

"Oops, sorry about that, kids. I must get more practice in with my landing. Are you both okay?" he asked, turning his head to check on them. Both Maddie and Theo were very disoriented after the bumpy landing.

The ride was glorious, and the light, breezy winds refreshed them as they flew high above the treetops. There were vast, hilly areas far on the horizon. Their beauty increased as they rose like magic. The grey mists of the evening were still clinging to the air when the three had taken off. It was a peaceful flight through the sky at night.

"Mr J, why can't you tell us about the quest and the bad news?" Maddie bugged him.

"You will have to wait until we are at Head Office, I'm afraid. The green men will explain it to you."

"But we want to know."

"Maddie, leave it. You need to be patient. All will be revealed. Relax and enjoy the ride," Mr J told her firmly. Maddie was cross, but she decided to shut up for now.

When they left the zoo for Head Office, Mr J's wings magically expanded. His whole body grew five times its original size, and a seat appeared on each wing for the children to sit on. Maddie looked at Theo in amazement as they clambered on and got comfortable. Mr J prepared for takeoff. It wasn't a very long journey, but it was such a huge zoo that it would take too much time to walk from place to place.

"Wowzeroney, Mr J! This place is something else, isn't it? Oooh, can we look around? It's so sparkly everywhere. I want to explore," Maddie exclaimed, as she tried to wander off, forgetting the whole point of the quest ahead of them.

"Maddie, my dear, we are here for a purpose, remember? Keep your focus, girl. Follow me! Come, come, children. This way." Mr J marched them straight to the main office.

Maddie was right, though. It sure was a spectacular place, like nothing they had ever seen before or could have imagined. Buildings of many colours were dotted about, but they didn't stay still. One minute they were there, solid and sturdy, and within seconds they changed shape and colour.

As Maddie glanced to her right, she noticed some buildings that looked like large, round glass balls. They were huge. Inside each ball was a forest.

"Look at those, Theo. Aren't they cool?" She pointed across to the glass balls as they disappeared from sight. She blinked and they turned into stairs. Maddie walked over to the bottom of the staircase and looked up. The stairs didn't go anywhere and within seconds they floated off into the air, replaced by a tall, looming building. It created a dark, scary shadow. Maddie was pleased when that changed yet again.

She looked down at the ground beneath them. It, too, appeared solid and concrete, but it moved constantly. One minute it was solid, and the next there were gaps. Maddie giggled.

"I can't keep up. I'm scared we are going to fall through the gaps." She grabbed hold of Theo to steady herself, hopping from one foot to the other.

It was all very magical and mystical, but they had to keep on their toes. Both children were super fascinated by it all. They jumped over the gaps. Maddie thought of it like the game she often played at home where they tried not to step on the cracks of the pavement slabs in the street.

Trucks rode past them too, but they didn't seem to be driving around the children. Rather, they drove through them, and although Maddie felt it, it didn't hurt. It merely felt fuzzy. This place was so bizarre.

The truck drivers were cute, funny little wizard-like creatures, green all over with squeaky voices and orange eyes. They smiled but continued with their work.

"Hurry along, children. We haven't got all night." Mr J complained. He was a funny dude, Mr J, but he also took his job seriously. He made it clear he wanted to get on with the quest as quickly as possible.

Within a few minutes, they reached one of the ever-changing buildings. They stepped inside, still mesmerised by the way of things in this strange place. Once they stepped inside, the building seemed to ground itself. Maddie made a mental note to ask Mr J if this always happened and whether this was the only way to keep them still.

As they entered Head Office, Maddie was amazed. "Wow," she said.

"Kids, this is Head Office. Meet the top bosses of this operation and listen carefully. They are the font of all knowledge—oh, yeah, you are young'uns. So, what that means is . . . umm, never mind. Let's crack on, shall we?" Mr J said.

They stood on a long orange carpet which stretched out before them for miles and miles. It wasn't carpet material as Maddie knew it. It was more like plastic. Above her, a huge round blue light dropped down so low it almost touched the top of her head. On each side of the carpet, she saw lots of wonky desks with matching chairs. The legs on the chairs were different sizes. Some were painted in green and yellow stripes, and some were painted in blue and orange dots.

The children sat down in the chairs. Maddie's chair leaned to the left, and she giggled as her whole body followed suit. She noticed Theo's chair leant forward. He didn't look comfortable. His feet were planted to the floor to stabilise him.

She stared at the two large green men standing in front of them. They had strange eyes. One rested higher than the other on each face. Both green men had the same eyes. They looked just like the little truck-driving men, only larger in size. They didn't look like bosses to Maddie. They looked more like cartoon characters.

The only difference between the two men was that one wore a blue hat. She was getting used to all the strange stuff now, though, so she chose to go along with it. It was fun.

The man who stood in front of them spoke. "Hello and welcome, kids. Thanks for coming to help us. This is going to be a tough quest we have on our hands, but I feel you two will be an asset to us. So, here is the deal . . ." He perched on the edge of one of the wonky chairs.

"A kakarooni has been taken hostage from the zoo. They can't survive without their special diet and cold climate for more than seventy-two hours. We need your help finding him and capturing the kidnapper. Now, let me explain our plan of action."

Both children wore dismayed expressions. "Oh, I thought we were here to do something fun." Maddie had not in the least expected this to be the quest. However, she felt a desperate urge to help get the kakarooni back to the zoo.

The large green man continued. "Our job here at Head Office is to oversee all that is going on in Kakarooni Zoo and make sure everything is okay. Through our camera system, we saw someone kidnap the kakarooni around six this evening."

Maddie gasped. "That's horrible. Who would do that?"

"Yes, it is. We think you would make great detectives to help us find him! Time is not on our side here, so we are going to have to move at a fast pace." He stood up and picked up a folder from the shelf behind him.

"Time here in Imagination World is very different anyway. You won't be missed back home. I have a few more instructions for you, and then we can begin," he said, opening the folder.

The other green man walked over to a nearby cupboard. When he returned, he handed a satchel to Theo.

"Look inside," he instructed. "There are some instruments. Look after these and use them when needed. You will know when that is."

There were also some magic sweets, which Theo was to distribute as he saw fit.

"Maddie, you are in charge of reminding Mr J to keep in contact with us." The first green man continued, flipping to the next page.

"The plan of action is to track down the kidnapper. Take the kakarooni ride to Rainbow Slide Park." He glanced at both children, took a sip of what Maddie assumed was coffee, and continued. Maddie tried not to giggle as she noticed a thin, frothy milk moustache had been left on the green man's top lip.

"I want you to make your way to Rainbow Slide Park first. I have a strong suspicion the kidnapper will head that way. It is an easy route out of the zoo." He paused and licked his lips, wiping away any trace of the milk moustache.

"The team here at Head Office is in the process of casting a spell on him. Now, are there any questions, or are you happy to get started?" he asked.

"Why can't you tell us where he is so we can go straight to him? Wouldn't that be easier?" Maddie asked.

"Yes, that is a great question. But we don't know where he is right now. He is running about all over the zoo, and it is massive here. If we spot him on camera or if anything comes up that we think will help you, we will be in touch."

Theo chimed in. "Why did you choose us? Did you make us meet at the railway station, then? Was this all a set-up?" He looked nervous. He spoke with a soft, quiet voice. Maddie watched his cheeks burn up and was sure she could hear his heart thudding. She knew how important it was for him to make sense of it all.

"Well, we have our reasons. You don't need to worry about that right now, young Theo. Right now, it's important that we can rely on you to help."

Theo shrugged his shoulders and smirked. "I guess so, sir."

The other green man with the blue hat piped up. "The sweets are magical. Please have one right now to perk you up and get you ready. Take one any time you feel tired. They are like a magic potion. We make them here on-site. They taste so nice. Try away, kids."

Maddie giggled, lent over towards Theo, and whispered in his ear. "I think we should call him Mr Blue Hat and the other one Green Wonky Eyes." Theo smiled and let out a little giggle too.

"So, are you ready to begin? This is going to be an amazing mission, kids, even though it may be tough in places. I can feel the strengths you both have within you to complete this and get our kakarooni back where he belongs. You have the makings of mini warriors." The first green man spoke again. "Please go and begin!"

• • •

Theo crossed his legs a little, trying to hold himself. They were back at the zoo now and had almost reached the toilet block. Maddie laughed at him.

"Are you doing the wee dance, Theo?" Her nose wrinkled, and her eyes narrowed when she got a fit of giggles. He looked away from her. She realised she had embarrassed him and felt a small pang of guilt.

There was a large toilet block to the left of the street food. Mr J told them he was leaving to call Head Office while they went to do all their necessary human things, most of which he didn't really understand and thought were pointless. But what did a Jamaican owl know, anyway?

Maddie surveyed the street food in front of them while she waited for Theo. There were three stalls. One offered Greek-style food, another Asian noodles, and the last one was a vegan stall. Her favourite was Greek. The smell made her feel a little hungry again.

Theo reappeared, still guarding the satchel with his life as he had since leaving Head Office. He refused to take it off. Maddie got the feeling he liked being important. They stopped at the Greek food stall and grabbed a couple of drinks while they waited for Mr J. Theo slurped his coke as he asked Maddie, "Where abouts do you live?"

"I live at the back of the railway with my aunt."

"Have you always lived with your aunt?"

"Since I was two, yes. My mum died giving birth to me, and my dad died when he fell off the roof when he was working. I don't know anything about them. I have a photograph at the side of my bed." She sighed.

"They look like they were kind people, and Aunt tells me they were. I think it upsets her too much to talk about them, so I don't ask."

Maddie stopped as the sadness overwhelmed her. Theo looked at her.

"I'm sorry to hear about your parents," he said.

"That's okay. I'm used to it. Where do you live?" she asked him.

"I live two streets away from the railway station, just the other side of the Hamilton Park. Do you know where I mean?"

"Oh yes, I love that park. Sometimes my cousin comes to visit, and we play there. Who do you live with?"

"My mum and my brother, Tim."

"What about your dad? Don't you have one?"

"Yes, but he and Mum split up a few months ago, so we moved to this area. He wasn't a very nice man to mum or us."

Maddie frowned. "That is sad. Do you miss him?" She reached over and squeezed his arm.

"Not really. My mum is happier now." He smiled.

They finished up their drinks, Maddie leaving the last bit of her hot chocolate drink as always. It had gotten dusky by the time they stepped away from the food stall to look out for Mr J.

"I wonder where . . . Oh, hello, Mr J. I was just thinking about where you were," Maddie said as he reappeared as if by magic. They were keen to get cracking now.

"Hi, kids. I have some information about the kidnapper," Mr J began.

"Oh, goody. We want to get on and help, don't we, Theo?" Maddie said and turned to him for a response. Theo nodded,

"Good. Well, firstly Head Office has spotted him on camera over by the helter-skelter. So, we need to get over there right away. Head Office thinks he is trying to get to the entrance of the zoo and escape. The zoo is large though, so there are plenty of places for him to hide."

"Let's go," Theo said, marching forward.

• • •

The air was fresh and warm for their walk across the zoo. It wasn't too far a trek from the food stalls. The faint smell of the last of the food that had been cooking all day floated around them. The birds had mellowed. All was peaceful and still this evening. They walked past another beautiful pond area and heard only the light trickling of the fountain as it tiptoed into the water. It was charming here now that it was deserted.

"Oh, it is all locked up." Maddie sighed as they reached the helter-skelter area. Her mouth curved downwards.

She could see a teacup ride, one of her favourite rides. She related it to that same dizzy feeling she felt on the roundabout.

"Oh, look. Go-karts. I love those." Theo pointed towards them. Maddie loved seeing Theo enthusiastic.

The rides were all tucked away in a fenced area and separate from the huge helter-skelter, which loomed over all the rides and cast a large shadow onto them. The entrance gate was locked. Theo and Maddie looked to Mr J for an answer.

In true Mr J style, he pondered for a moment, scratching his feathers as an act of habit when deep in thought.

"Never fear for Mr J is here," he said. "Although, yes, it is all locked up. Umm, hang on a minute. I have an idea." With that, he toddled off. Theo and Maddie watched him. He walked all the way round to the back of the fence. It wasn't very high at all, so they could see every move he made.

Within a few minutes, they could hear him whistling and chattering to himself. He had burrowed his way to the inside. He must have been feeling very pleased with himself. He sauntered over to the gate and unlocked it from inside.

"Please enter at your own peril, dear children," he said to them, laughing his little shaved pink head off whilst holding the gate open for them.

They were a little too young to get his sense of humour, but they knew what he meant.

"Remember, we are here to see if the kidnapper is here or has been here. We mustn't forget our quest," he reminded them with a stern tone. They both nodded, eager to get on. Maddie knew that meant they couldn't mess about or play.

"Mr J, what does the kidnapper look like? There doesn't seem to be anyone here, especially a man with a kakarooni. Wouldn't we have seen him already?" Maddie asked. She looked around herself. It was deserted. Head Office had shown Mr J a picture when he called them for information. But he did not have the photo with him, so he did his best to describe the man to the children.

"He is not very tall, and he has dark hair, dark eyes. His eyebrows are thick and bushy. He has a moustache and a little goatee beard. He has a serious look about his face, a constant frown." He thought for a moment before continuing.

"Little pointy ears and a long nose. He has a scar on the right side of his neck. It looks like a knife wound. He is fairly muscly too."

"Oh, my teacher has a moustache. They look like dead caterpillars to me." She giggled. "Okay, we will keep our eyes peeled then, Mr J." She had often heard her aunt use this phrase. She found it hilarious. *Who would peel their own eyes?* She thought and chuckled to herself as she did every time she heard it.

"Children, I have to pop into the control box. Head Office thought they saw the kidnapper messing around in there, so there could be a clue. We can't leave anything to chance. When I get back, we can continue looking for him. Come on, you can come with me and help me look."

They checked all around the control box but found no sign of any clues. Just as they were about to leave, Mr J shuddered.

"I think something brushed past my shoulder. Did you two feel that?" he asked as he spun around quickly to see who was there. No one. But then a voice spoke to them.

Maddie could barely make out a black-and-grey shadow of smoke like a wispy ghost. He had shiny white eyes that looked straight through her. He floated and hovered over the controls. Theo saw it too and clung to Maddie.

"I am Brazi, king of the adninjas. You have missed the kidnapper. You will always be one step behind him. He has an advantage over you. Get your children and come fight us." He swished his wispy body up above them and floated out of the side window.

"You will not get to the kidnapper unless you get past us first! Come to the go-karts. My adninja team awaits." Then he was gone.

• • •

"Let's go fight them. I'm not afraid of wispy smoke people," Maddie announced, hand on hip, a serious glare in her eyes.

She grabbed Theo's hand and marched to the go-karts. Her confidence was overpowering. She saw the fear in Theo's eyes.

"We will look after you, Theo. I promise."

The go-karts were a little further round, past the caterpillar rollercoaster and the giant water slide. They were parked exactly beneath the helter-skelter. By now the sky was dark with a few stars sprinkled about. A jet engine rumbled faintly in the distance. Maddie looked up and saw the white line streaked across the sky. She was mesmerised by the stars, which were so clear tonight.

"I'm a little nervous, Maddie," Theo said. She held him tight and felt him shaking.

"You have me." She smiled. He smiled back as her gaze left the starry sky and returned back to the moment in front of her.

As they neared the go-karts, Maddie couldn't see anyone or anything resembling a wispy shadow. She wondered if they had decided against a fight. If so, she knew Theo would be happy. The least Maddie wanted to do was find out what advantage the kidnapper had over them.

With a sudden deep roar and bright white flashing lights, the go-karts came to life. The music played, and the go-karts zoomed around the course, crashing into each other. One empty kart sat motionless on the side. A large neon light above it flashed the words "Maddie & Theo." They looked at one another, and even Theo knew what they had to do.

Mr J cheered them on from the sidelines as they strapped themselves in and awaited instructions. King Brazi swooped into the middle of the go-kart track. He swayed in midair, pushed his wispy arms out in front of himself, and shouted, "Listen up. The aim of the game is to take all the other go-karts out. You have two minutes. Go!"

Maddie could now see all the adninjas. Under the lights, they became visible. She could hear them cackling.

The battle commenced. Maddie drove the go-kart. It was mayhem. The king stayed in his floating position. He shouted once more. "If you win, I will tell you why the kidnapper has an advantage. If you lose, there will be another battle to face."

Maddie and Theo knew they had to defeat these horrid wispy creatures with their deadly white shining eyes.

After one minute a buzzer sounded, and the king shouted, "Half-time!"

Maddie drove like a wild child. She was super determined to take them all out. Theo had his hands over his eyes for most of the time. She wasn't a careful driver at all. When they hit another go-kart, the adninja flew from its seat and splat on the ground. It was pretty good fun. There was only one adninja per kart. So far Maddie had splatted four of them with six left to knock out in the last minute. Her face full of concentration, she pressed her foot harder on the gas pedal.

Maddie heard King Brazi laugh as he thought she was going to fail, but right in the last few seconds Theo took control of the wheel and smashed into the last go-kart with such force and determination that no one would have had a chance at survival. Maddie and Mr J were both shocked, yet they were super proud of him. It sure wiped the smile off the king's face.

As they left the go-kart arena, Maddie gave Theo a massive hug. "You were so awesome. We would never have won if you didn't take the wheel. I am so proud of you." She kissed his cheek and felt the warm glow of his embarrassment. He didn't respond. He only gave a little shrug.

"Well, well, well. I am shocked you won. I have misjudged you by a long shot and given you too easy a battle. I will not make this mistake again, never fear. You did win fair and square though. However, when we meet again you will not defeat me!" King Brazi did not look like a happy wispy smoke-person. His voice was full of anger, his shiny white eyes even bulgier than before. Maddie thought he looked like he was going to explode, if that was even possible for such a non-solid sort of person. She guessed he expected them to fail.

"Hah, I'm glad we won," Maddie replied. "We will never let you beat us. We are going to find that kidnapper and make him return the kakarooni. You just watch. Now, tell us why he has an advantage. You promised," she shouted, pouting her lips.

"I will tell you, but I promise that was a super easy battle for you to win. I will not be so naive next time." He floated close to Maddie's face. His breath smelt stale and made her heave.

"The kidnapper has a superpower. He can turn into anything he wants. He can become an adninja or a tree or a rock or any other animal or creature he chooses, so you will never find him. It will be impossible because you are looking for a man, and he will never show himself as a man." The king threw his head back in laughter as he explained.

"Well, you are wrong because Head Office saw him on their camera," Maddie argued.

"His superpower has only recently kicked in, so he will have been seen on camera," King Brazi replied. "His superpower comes from the kakarooni. The kakaroonis are awesome creatures as you well know. Some of them have built-in superpowers. You can tell which ones by looking them in the eye. So, keep trying, children. But you will never defeat him. I am done here. I'll see you at the next task. I can assure you it won't be so easy."

And with that, the king disappeared into the night. All that was left behind was the faint echo of his laughter.

CHAPTER 4

The Kakarooni Ride

"Good night, Mr J. Thank you for reading to us and making us comfy. Are you going to Head Office now?" Maddie asked. He had just settled them in for the night. They were going to sleep in the Cold Library on the hay bales. Mr J had found some blankets for them, so they snuggled up in these.

"Yes, I am. A Jamaican owl doesn't need to sleep. Well, not how you humans do anyway," he explained.

"What do you mean?" she asked, sitting herself back up.

"Well, Jamaican owls can nap when they need to in between other daytime tasks. It's all we need. Now, come on and get to sleep. I am going to see what the latest information is, and I will be back in the morning to fill you in. Sleep tight, both of you." He pecked a little kiss onto Maddie's head and said ciao to Theo.

"Good night, Maddie," Theo whispered. "I'm very tired after all the excitement of today. Do you think we will catch the kidnapper? I want to get home as soon as we can." Maddie could hear the uncertainty in his voice.

"Go to sleep, Theo. It will all be okay. We have Mr J with us, and look how well we did with the go-karts. Don't worry. Good night." She closed her eyes and soon drifted off.

• • •

Maddie woke first. It took her a few minutes to remember where she was. She felt a piece of straw stuck to her arm. Her makeshift bed was warm and snuggly. It was comfortable sleeping on the bales. She saw Theo a few feet away from her on his own bale. He was still sound asleep. His hair was a little matted to his face, and she noticed his little nostrils flared and deflated in sync with his light snoring. He looked comfortable and peaceful under his blanket.

After the excitement of the go-karts, they were both tired-out. They had a long, tiring day all-round. So, Mr J suggested they got some sleep for a few hours and continue their search in the morning with fresh thoughts and ideas. He then took them back to the Cold Library, the only place in the zoo with a roof. So, even though it was kept cold for the kakaroonis, it was the best option. The building itself was large. It only had that one room in it apart from the entrance area where they had queued for the kakarooni food.

After the zoo closed, all the kakaroonis were taken back to their cages to sleep, so it was empty in the library. The room itself was basic. It consisted of bales of hay, chairs, and four bookshelves. Nothing else. The bookshelves were shoved into the back corner on the left. There were all sorts of books on them. The room itself was quiet. Natural light flooded in through two large patio doors. It was enough to wake Maddie.

Maddie loved reading, and since Theo was still asleep and Mr J was nowhere in sight, she wandered over to the bookshelves. She stretched her slim body, trying to wake herself up a little bit. A shiver crept over her as she jumped down from the hay and landed on the cold tiles. She pulled her cardigan tight around herself, easing the chill she felt from the room, and slipped her shoes on.

As she neared the bookshelf, her thoughts turned to King Brazi and what he had said about the kidnapper.

His superpower will always keep him one step ahead of us.

She didn't know an awful lot about superpowers, but she guessed there must be some way to stamp it out of him. If only they could figure this out.

The first bookshelf she came to had lots of children's books on it. Some were novels, some were colouring books, and some were picture books. There were also some puzzle-solving books. She thought of Theo and how much he would love these. She also wondered when Mr J would return. Sifting through the novels she came across one titled *The Snow Lady*. This title intrigued her. The picture on the front showed a lady who looked like a princess. The image only showed her back as she walked through the woods. She had long brown hair, but the rest of her person was made of snow, and she held a lacy umbrella in her right hand. Her dress was a mix of snow and leaves. Her left hand held a beautiful turquoise feather. It all looked so magical. She hoped Theo stayed asleep for a while so she could read this book.

Maddie made her way back to her hay bed and tucked herself under the blanket. She felt cosy and even warm as she lost herself in the pages of the book.

• • •

"Maddie, it's nine o clock already," Theo announced. She looked over at him. He looked like he had the weight of the world on his shoulders. She sat up on her bale of hay.

"Are you okay, Theo?" she asked him. Mr J woke them both half an hour before. Maddie had fallen back to sleep while reading her book. But she managed to read two chapters, and she really enjoyed it. She asked Mr J if she could keep it. He said no. However, she hoped they would be able to come back to the library later on. So, she pretended to place it back on the shelf but snuck it underneath and around the back of the bookcase, hiding it from view.

"I keep thinking about my mum. Do you think she is worried about me and where I am?" Theo asked.

"No, I don't. Time here is different, remember? You are worrying for nothing. Come on, Theo. You know it will all be okay. Let's go find Mr J. I think he is waiting for us outside." Maddie was losing her patience with him, but she still wanted to be kind.

It was a beautiful spring morning once again. The sky was a perfect shade of blue with not a cloud in sight. A slight chill swept through the air. They could hear the kakaroonis singing in their cages. The children sat in a small cafe just outside the Cold Library. Mr J was treating them to breakfast. They tucked into crispy bacon sandwiches. Maddie added a huge dollop of red sauce to hers. A small dot of sauce clung to the corner of her mouth.

"Head Office has informed me that the kidnapper is heading for Rainbow Slide Park again," Mr J said. "It will take him a while to get there because the zoo is so big, and the kidnapper doesn't know his way around it."

"Does this mean we can catch up with him, then?" Maddie asked as she licked the sauce away.

"We have a good chance, yes. Head Office plans to put many traps in his way. But he is sneaky, of course, and he has his superpower." Mr J lowered his voice. "I also suspect that King Brazi is helping him out a lot."

Once they finished eating, Mr J jumped off the table and into Maddie's lap.

"Please lower me to the floor, child. We need to head to the kakarooni ride. It will take us to the other side of the zoo, as close as possible to Rainbow Slide Park."

"My teeth feel horrible. It's bad enough wearing these smelly clothes, but I hate not brushing my teeth," Maddie told them. She was trying to smooth them over and release some of the trapped food by swishing her tongue across them.

Theo, on the other hand, didn't seem to care about his teeth or smelly clothes.

"Right then, kids. Shall we get moving? This way," Mr J said, beckoning them to follow him.

It wasn't very far to walk across to the entrance for the kakarooni ride, so they made their way over. Mr J wanted to get there before the queues started. The ride was always very popular. The payment desk for any of the rides in the zoo was located just to the right-hand side of the ride, so Mr J hopped away to go and purchase their tickets. Theo and Maddie sat on the ground, forming the beginning of the queue.

Theo looked over at Maddie. "What?" she asked as she caught him staring at her. He had a sneaky look about him.

For once, his cheeks didn't burn up. He appeared more relaxed. Maddie was sure he was becoming more comfortable around her.

"I was thinking about how confident you are, and I wanted to ask... are you scared of anything?"

Before responding, Maddie sat with her thoughts for a few moments. *Did she really come across that confident?*

She didn't see herself that way at all. After all, she was afraid of the dark, but she did see that she had learnt to become independent. She tried to see it from Theo's point of view. To her, Theo was quite a shy, timid boy. This was never a problem to her. She understood that everyone was different, and she thought it was an endearing quality. But she could understand that she would seem confident through his eyes. They were very different in character—of that she was certain. She wasn't ready to admit to him about her fear of the dark though, not yet.

"Yeah, I suppose I am quite confident. I don't know any other way. My aunt is quite old, so I often look after myself. She isn't very well a lot of the time. She has problems inside her head. She gets upset a lot, so I have to help her a lot with things." She tapped her head by way of explanation. Then she crossed her arms as she carried on.

"I always talk to people when we go shopping, and I've learnt to do things around the house. I'm not afraid of much." She brushed off the last statement in a rush. She hoped Theo wouldn't ask anything more about her fears. She continued before he had a chance to respond.

"I speak fluent Spanish, you know! Bet you are impressed now," she added, sticking out her tongue. She felt great about that. She knew she was quite clever in that way and hoped it would add to the things Theo liked about her.

"Wow, can you really?" His eyes spoke volumes. He moved a little closer to her.

"Yes, of course. Can you speak any languages?" she asked him. He grew shy again as he replied.

"No, but I can play the guitar. Do you like music?" Theo asked. His eyes widened as he spoke. "I love music. I always feel nice when I play or listen." Maddie loved listening to him talk. His face lit up when he talked about music. She could tell he was passionate about it.

"Yeah, I love music! I love singing along and dancing. It always makes me feel so good. My favourite band is The Backstreet Boys. Who do you like?" She asked, excited that they had something in common here.

They continued their conversation for a few minutes, each of them confessing their secret crushes in the music world. Theo was even brave enough to tell her how much he loved Taylor Swift. It was rare he admitted that to anyone. He confessed it was his guilty pleasure.

By the time Mr J returned, the queue had grown full of children excited to go on the ride. Maddie was especially excited for the ride ahead.

"Will the ride take us straight to Rainbow Slide Park?" she asked Mr J.

She loved the sound of Rainbow Slide Park. She could imagine it would be such a fun place to play with bright, beautiful colours everywhere.

"Yes, it will," he assured her. "It's a long ride though."

Theo and Maddie chose a seat at the back. They settled themselves in, Theo of course clutching his satchel while Maddie didn't have a care in the world. She was excited about their next adventure onboard this ride. Her face shone, and she kept giggling. It looked like it would be fun in the back row.

The ride was a huge vehicle shaped like a kakarooni, and all the seats were rainbow-coloured. Some were shaped like kakarooni feet, and some resembled their large puppy dog eyes. The driver was dashing, dressed in colourful clothing and full of the joys of spring. He looked to Maddie like he loved his job.

"All aboard, kids! Come on, take your seats. We ain't got all day, you know! I am Paul, your captain for today's ride." Maddie could see the back of him from where she sat and watched his shoulders move up and down. She could hear him chuckling to himself.

Mr J settled himself in next to the kids. Several kakaroonis jumped onto the ride as well.

The ride was indescribable, and each round was different. It was as if magic occurred behind the scenes. The ride started off slowly on a roller coaster track with twists and turns, and it even went upside down in places. There were screams of fear and excitement as the roller coaster neared the top of the incline. The kids waited in anticipation, not knowing what to expect next.

Just as they thought they would career down the track at high speed, they flew straight off the track and into the air as the kakarooni vehicle morphed into a hot air balloon.

"Wow!" Maddie exclaimed. It wasn't often she was at a loss for words, but the magic of the ride had taken her by surprise. It was so peaceful up in the air too, so still and calm, and one could see for miles and miles around.

The passengers were silent as everyone soaked up the experience. The feeling in the balloon was gorgeous. Even the kakaroonis felt peaceful.

A moment later the balloon whooshed down into the beautiful rainbow-sparkled lake below. Once again, the kakarooni vehicle changed. This time it took the form of a cute little boat split into different boats—canoes and kayaks. They were all one boat and all separate at the same time. Theo, Maddie, and Mr J found themselves in a canoe-style boat.

Similar to the hot air balloon, the canoe ride brought them peacefully across the tranquil lake. Nature made the only sounds, chattering in its own magical way through the whispers of the trees which drooped over the lake. Birds in the sky uttered beautiful chirps and tweets. And, of course, the fresh water rippled beneath them.

The kakaroonis jumped into the water and played with all the sea animals. There were dolphorses, crocozebs, and unicwhales.

"Look at these amazing animals," Maddie chirped, disturbing everyone's peace. "The dolphorses look like a mixture of dolphins and horses. Isn't this so amazing, Theo? I could stay on the ride all day long." She loved watching the kakaroonis playing with all the sea animals. Everything was so magical in Kakarooni Zoo.

"Yes, it's so great here, isn't it?" Theo replied, staring blissfully into space. "I want to stay forever—not only on the ride, but in the zoo. It's all so magical in this world, so beautiful. The crocozebs are like crocodiles, but striped. And those unicwhales are lovely. They look like whales with a bit of unicorn thrown in."

After letting the animals play together for about five minutes, Paul rounded them all up to get back on board as they were off for the next part of the adventure. All the animals jumped back into the boats, and by sheer magic more boats appeared so the unicwhales could join for the rest of the ride, too.

Once everyone was back in their seats, settled down and comfortable, Paul started up the boat's engine and shouted "Close your eyes, everyone. The magic will happen only if we are all the same. Get ready for it!" Maddie adored the excitement she heard in his voice.

The boat took off nice and gentle to start with. It glided across the water for a few minutes until suddenly it whooshed back up into the air, and they were flying high above the trees again. This time the boat changed into a giant albatross. Albatrosses were known for their huge wingspan, so they were all strapped in across his wings, soaring higher and higher into the sky.

"This is your captain speaking," Mr Albatross said loudly. "We have such a clear, stunning day today, so we are very lucky to be able to fly high and feel the beauty of the open air. After three I want you all to shout 'wee' at the tops of your voices... ready? One, two, three..."

Everyone played along and joined in. The air of excitement amongst them all was clear from their shouts of glee. Off they soared all over the place, flying round and round. They could see the zoo below and all the other children and kakaroonis looking up at them in amazement. The zoo was full of people now. This ride lasted a long time. Maddie loved it, although she was also anxious to get to Rainbow Slide Park and crack on with catching the kidnapper. But she stayed in the moment and enjoyed it for what it was.

They flew over the tops of trees and amongst the other birds. They flew past the highest of buildings, staring straight into office windows at the hard workers. But the main attraction was flying in the open air with nothing around but the pure beauty of the sky, the glorious weather, and all the natural world. It smelt crisp and fresh all around.

The unicwhales sat next to Maddie, Theo, and Mr J. They always loved a cuddle and always liked to tell a story or give a running commentary of where one was headed as one travelled across the zoo. They behaved like typical tour guides.

On this occasion, there were three unicwhales onboard, which Maddie revelled at, pointing out that Theo, Mr J, and she could all have a cuddle and a tour guide. The simplest of things sure did please her.

All three unicwhales told the children a story of the zoo. They took it in turns to say a sentence each. It was such a clever, well-planned idea. They were in sync with each other, knowing when one would end their part or pick up the next line. Just like the kakaroonis, they spoke in English. The kids were amazed by this, and their eyes locked on the unicwhales with wonder.

Mincha, Artcru, and Dhow adored telling a good story, never quite knowing whether they were making it up or not. It was a magical place, and enchanted things always happened. They couldn't control what came out of their mouths next.

"And over here to the left is where Kakarooni Zoo was first thought about," Mincha explained, pointing towards the kakarooni trees.

"By the great kakarooni king—Sir Kakaralite. He was the ultimate founder," Artcru continued.

"He was half-kakarooni, half-human." Dhow chipped in, ending the commentary.

All too soon it was time for the ride to come to an end. As they descended, the albatross seemed to melt away beneath them and return to its kakarooni form just in time to hit the track and roll along to the end, coming to a quick, sharp stop.

"That's it, guys. Hope you enjoyed it. Woohoo! I sure did, as always. See you again soon," Paul said as the ride jolted to a halt. His enthusiasm never died through the whole ride.

As everyone chatted amongst themselves, waiting to disembark, Maddie watched Paul. He looked uncomfortable. His face had taken on a frown, and she saw him staring out of his window with worry. His fingers rested on his chin as he stared straight ahead. She sensed something wasn't right. Although she had not been to Rainbow Slide Park before, looking out of the window, she didn't feel this was the right place.

"Okay, you lovely lot, it seems things haven't quite gone according to plan," Paul said. "I don't understand exactly what has happened here, but we haven't landed in Rainbow Slide Park. I'm going to leave you all inside for a minute while I try to figure this out." He opened his side door and slipped through it. It locked behind him.

From where they were seated, Maddie could still see Paul. He was strolling about down the side of the ride. The last thing she heard was a scream as he was sucked into a black, grey, and wispy void. A horrid knot formed inside Maddie's tummy as she realised the king and his adninjas were back.

• • •

"Oh no, Mr J, look out the window," Maddie exclaimed. "Paul has disappeared, and the adninjas are back. What are we going to do?"

Theo and Mr J couldn't see from where they were seated. Mr J jumped up onto Maddie's shoulder to get a better view. There wasn't anything to be seen now, though, as Paul had disappeared.

"Umm, it seems we may have another adninja battle on our hands, children," Mr J replied, jumping back down and considering his next plan of action. He waddled over to the unicwhales and untangled them from the children and their cuddles.

"Any advice, you three?" he asked Mincha, Artcru, and Dhow.

The unicwhales began to think of a solution. Dhow suggested they try the doors—maybe they would open. It didn't work.

There were six other passengers on the ride besides Maddie, Theo, Mr J, and of course the unicwhales and kakaroonis. None were adults. Mr J wanted to get them all out and send them back to their parents.

Everyone was busy trying to figure out how to get the doors open. The front carriage where Paul had sat and operated the ride was separate from the main carriage. Maddie tried the door to the front carriage, but it was also locked. Theo opened his window and shouted out to King Brazi. He could almost see him floating about. He was difficult to make out in the light of day.

"Oi, Mr King Brazi, let us out of here. What's going on?" His braveness began to shine through yet again.

"No chance. I told you I would up my game. I gave you an easy task, and now you have paid for it. Don't cross me again. You will never get to my master, and even if you do, the stakes have now risen," he shouted. Then he floated closer to the window.

"He told me to inform you that the money has doubled. Give up while you still can. You will never make it to Rainbow Slide Park!" Theo sunk in his seat. Maddie watched the king fade into the distance, leaving them trapped.

CHAPTER 5

Mincha, Artcru, Dhow, and the Flower Gardens

"What are we going to do? How are we going to get out now?" Without waiting for an answer, Maddie slammed her arms into the air and ran to the doors. She tugged on the main door, but it wouldn't budge. She kicked and spun around, punching the wall before collapsing into a heap on the floor. Clutching her head in her hands, she sobbed.

Theo ran over and placed his warm hand on her arm.

"Maddie, it's okay. I have an idea. Remember, we have the satchel. There is a magic wand inside it." He pulled it out from the bag and waved it in front of her face. Maddie wiped her damp eyes with the back of her hands and looked up at him.

Mr J waddled over to them. "Good man, Theo. Let's crack on and get out of here, then, shall we?"

"But how do we know how to make it work?" Maddie asked between sobs. Theo felt her pain. He hated to feel trapped.

"Well, well, young Maddie. I reckon it won't take much figuring out. Stand back here out of the way. Theo, are you feeling brave, young man?" Mr J asked as he helped Maddie to her feet.

"Yes, Mr J. I can do this." Theo pointed the wand at the main door. His hands clutched it tight. Mr J jumped up onto his shoulder. Theo felt strong and powerful as he took a long, deep breath. He had no idea where this strength came from.

"Open sesame," he shouted. His face bore a deep frown. His body stiffened. His fingers wrapped around the wand so hard he thought he might squeeze the life from it. Everyone waited in complete silence. Nothing happened.

Theo tried again. He gripped the wand tighter and steadied his feet. Mr J whispered in his ear, "You've got this, boy."

"Open sesame," he shouted, louder this time. Maddie's jaw dropped as the wand took on a life of its own. It spun out of Theo's hands with a heavy force, smacked into the door, and fell to the floor. As it hit the ground, a bright light shone from it. It illuminated the entire door frame as the door swung open in slow motion.

Theo was rooted to the spot.

"Yippee, Theo!" Maddie ran forward and squeezed him. Mr J hurried them all along.

"Let's go," he said as he ushered them one by one through the door. Just before he and Theo tumbled through the door, Theo bent down and picked up the wand. But it burnt his hand. He dropped it as it burst into flames. Mr J grabbed Theo, and they dived through the open door just in time. They landed in a heap on the grass. Maddie ran over to them, screaming. Theo looked up and watched the kakarooni ride burn in front of them.

• • •

"I'm so glad you remembered the satchel, Theo. I think we would have been stuck inside the kakarooni ride forever." Maddie stroked his arm. She was gentle with him. Her face lit up as she smiled.

Maddie, Theo, and Mr J all sat on the riverbank. They had ended up in a flower garden. It was set around a beautiful river, which curved in a soft path through the trees. White blossoms lay across the tips of the trees. It was a spectacular sight. The colours of the flowers were so vibrant, and the smell was so sweet. All the different flowers together created such beauty. There were blues, reds, yellows, pinks, purples, peaches, and everything in between. An older couple on the opposite side strolled hand in hand along the woodland pathway.

In the distance, Theo could hear the faint hum of a tractor. There were a few fields off to the left, and as it was springtime, he knew farmers were busy harvesting their crops. It was a nice sound, peaceful, and full of new life.

"Yes, I'm glad too. That magic wand was so clever," Theo replied.

Maddie's nostrils expanded as she sniffed the air. It was fresh, light, and floral—a sure sign the flowers were blossoming in their beautiful setting. Theo saw a bridge in the distance. It arched over the river, hugging it tight. The unicwhales lazed about nearby. It turned out to be a gorgeous sunny day. He watched Mincha tiptoe over to the river's edge and take a few sips of the crystal-clear water. She was such a delicate creature. In fact, all three of them were.

They all felt a little deflated and decided to rest a little while and take in the beauty of the nature around them. Nature always seemed to provide a sense of freedom which helped them relax and clear their minds.

Theo decided to brave it and took his satchel off his shoulder, but he kept his hand closed around the strap. He held on tight while it lay beside him on the grass. He then entered a deep conversation with Mr J. Maddie moved closer to the boys and listened.

"I feel like we are losing control." Mr J moaned. "The kidnapper and Brazi always seem to be one step ahead. I thought we were gaining on them after defeating them at the go-karts. We need to up our game."

The unicwhales decided they would stick around with the children and Mr J. They wanted to help in any way they could.

"I have an idea," Theo said to Mr J. "We will not let the king and his team stop us."

• • •

Theo shuffled over to Mincha, Artcru, and Dhow. They were still lazing about in the sunshine. They looked like they were enjoying themselves. Unicwhales tend to be lazy. Theo loved how they were such beautiful creatures. Half unicorn and half whale. Perhaps a little more whale, hence them living in the water most of the time. There's a smoothness to their blue skin. But the most beautiful part is their unicorn horn. It is rainbow-coloured—peculiar, yet subtle. It shines and sparkles. Theo was particularly mesmerised by their eyes. They were a rare aqua green colour.

"What can we do to help them more? I feel useless." Theo overheard them talking amongst themselves. They were such kind, loving creatures.

They had lived in Kakarooni Zoo all their lives, and a kidnapping had never happened before. However, they did know the zoo inside out and back to front. Artcru noted that it would take a long time to get to Rainbow Slide Park from here. The kakarooni ride would have been perfect had it worked out as planned. The ride was made for such a trip.

Theo plonked himself down next to them and didn't interrupt.

"Don't forget the secret passages," Dhow reminded the others. "They aren't always visible, and they aren't often straightforward or accessible. Sometimes there are clues and puzzles one must solve to get through such passages."

"Yes, of course. We should tell the children and Mr J. It might help them get to the kidnapper faster."

Theo was fascinated by what he heard. "We need to go. Mr J and I have come up with a plan," he explained to them.

The three of them scrambled up onto their bellies and rolled themselves up onto their feet. It was a sight! They weren't very used to being on the ground and having legs to use. Theo thought it was hilarious. He couldn't help but let out a little giggle, but he covered his mouth with his hand, trying to tame it.

Mr J spoke as they all huddled together. "So, the clever Theo here and my good, wise owl self have an idea. We want to run it past you all and hear your ideas, too, of course, should you wish to share and help."

The unicwhales sat close, ears poised and ready. Maddie did too. Theo felt Maddie's eyes on him and wondered what she was thinking. More than likely, this was the reason he wasn't as confident as she was.

"We thought we could go and rescue the kakarooni ride," Theo said. "We could have a go at saving it and then get ourselves to Rainbow Slide Park. How hard can it be?"

"That's a great plan. There is a team of us, and I'm sure Head Office can help somehow. They seem to be able to do magical things." Maddie was full of enthusiasm as always. However, the unicwhales looked at one another and then at the other three.

"Now wait a minute," Mincha piped up. "We don't mean to be negative or anything, but no one here has any clue how to fix a ride that has fire damage. We would need the fire brigade to help. We have a much better idea."

Everyone listened eagerly as Mincha continued.

"We know this zoo pretty well, and there are secret passages dotted about."

Maddie's eyes lit up at the potential excitement of this.

"Oh, wow, secret passages! How exciting. Can we fix the ride and use the secret passages?" she asked Mr J.

"It sure is a possibility," he agreed.

Much to the unicwhales' disappointment, they all marched off in the direction of the kakarooni ride. Mr J suggested they could at least go and check it out and see what they were up against.

It wasn't a long walk to the place where the ride landed, and it involved a beautiful stroll through the gardens. They walked in the direction of the bridge. They crossed the bridge, and then it was a short walk to the river bend. As the river bent off to the left, there was a huge field scattered with fresh seeds of crops.

Maddie stopped for a second at a gorgeous yellow flower. It popped out from all the wildflowers on the edge of the riverbank. It was a poppy just like the one they had been eyeing up at the railway station.

"Look, Theo," she said as she reached out to touch the poppy. The petals looked smooth and delicate, yet wispy. "It's another yellow poppy. I love these flowers."

Before she had a chance to say anything further, Dhow grabbed her hand. "Don't touch those poppies, Maddie!" she snapped and glared at Maddie, her eyes boring into her.

"Why not?"

"You have to trust me. It isn't important for you to know right now. Don't touch them. Come on, we need to get to the kakarooni ride."

Maddie let it go although Theo could sense how much she wanted to know about the yellow poppies. As Dhow joined the other unicwhales, Maddie and Theo walked behind them. Theo chuckled as she stuck her tongue out at Dhow, but Mr J caught her out of the corner of his eye. He raised an eyebrow but said nothing.

Maddie was lagging behind in her carefree way. Theo stopped to wait for her.

"Come on, Maddie."

Maddie stopped in her tracks and threw her hands in the air. "I really want to know about the yellow poppy. I bet it is something exciting," she said.

"Well, whatever it is, I'm sure we will know in good time. Aren't you excited to get the ride up and running?" he asked. It was all he could think about. He didn't understand why Maddie was so easily distracted. He took her hand and led her forward.

"Yeah, I suppose so," she answered, stepping in line with him.

They reached the broken ride after a few more minutes. It didn't look half as bad as Theo remembered it. He was sure it had been a lot worse, much more burnt out.

After they all stood and stared for a few minutes, Artcru broke the silence. "Well, I reckon it looks fixable. We simply need to clean up all the ash, and as long as there are some seats for us all, we can make the ride start. What more is there to do?"

The flames hadn't lasted very long by the looks of it, but the ride was covered in black ash. It sure wasn't as bad as they had thought it would be. Some of the seats had burnt out. The roof had gone altogether, as had the left-hand side, though only part the way down. It would be a breezy ride if they did manage to get it working.

"But will it be okay without a roof and sides? Won't it be all wobbly?" Maddie asked. Her face screwed up.

"Well, all we can do is try," Artcru replied with her gorgeous eyes sparkling at Maddie. She was right. They had nothing to lose and everything to gain. It would be great to get it up and running again not only for transporting them to Rainbow Slide Park. It was also a fabulous ride for the zoo.

They all decided Mr J would be the best candidate to see if the engine would start. The others all began to clean up as best they could.

"We don't have anything to clean with," Maddie said.

"Well, how about we use leaves off the trees," Theo suggested. "They might work like cloths."

"Yes, what a great idea," Maddie said as she and Theo wandered off to collect as many as they could find. They all got to work scrubbing as much and as hard as they could to clean up the ride.

Meanwhile, Mr J went to the front cabin area where all the controls for the ride were, trying to start it up. He wasn't having much luck.

• • •

Maddie and Theo worked together at the back of the ride, cleaning up all the seats while the unicwhales cleaned up at the front. Mr J decided to open the engine. It looked very similar to that of a regular car's engine, and he spent a while tinkering about with it. He looked like he knew what he was looking for.

Maddie rubbed her tummy, and Theo heard it rumble with hunger.

"I'm hungry," she announced. He felt hungry himself.

"You are always hungry," he replied, smiling at her.

It was nearing lunchtime. Theo was surprised she hadn't moaned before now about wanting food. They had all been so engrossed in wanting to get this ride up and running.

Maddie waltzed off towards Mr J.

Theo halted his cleaning for a moment and watched Mincha sit down. He thought something was wrong but realised she looked tired out. They weren't used to this much work. Their usual day consisted of lazing about. He walked towards her, and as he did he noticed something on the seat opposite her.

"Mincha, what is that?" He pointed to a small parcel.

"I don't know. Let's see," she said, reaching over and picking it up. It was wrapped up like a birthday present, square in shape and tied up with a yellow ribbon. Nobody else had noticed as they were all still busy with their own tasks.

Mincha ripped it open. Inside was a brooch. It rested on beautiful pale pink-coloured paper. It was a gorgeous pendant in the shape of a peacock feather, blue and green with a diamond eye in the centre. As she lifted the brooch out of its box, she saw a note underneath it. It read:

I am your access through the secret passages. Whoever wears me will be the first to enter. Others can go with you, but you must all hold hands. You need to return to the flower garden. Take a left and walk along the riverbank. You will find the bridge on your right-hand side. You must walk until you have counted ten willow trees on your

side of the river. After this, the flower garden takes a twist. You will
see when you reach it. There is a secret passage here. You must look
carefully, and it will be revealed. Follow this, and you will soon end
up in Rainbow Slide Park.

Mincha jumped out of her seat.

"We should tell the others," she said. Theo nodded and shouted for everyone's attention. They all gathered around as Mincha showed them the brooch and the note.

"Hang on a minute," Mr J piped up. His stare was intense.

"Who would put that brooch and note here? Surely if it were Head Office, they would have told me. I don't think we should believe or follow this without checking. I am going to call Head Office to see what they know about it." He walked away, his eyes narrow. His whole little body was rigid as he moved. He looked almost wooden.

Theo agreed with Mr J. He was also suspicious and didn't believe it could be that easy. They all agreed that Mr J should at least call Head Office and see what they had to say about it all.

"I hope it is true. I'm so excited to go and play in the secret passages." Maddie grinned.

• • •

When Mr J returned, he announced that Head Office had confirmed it was them who had sent the brooch. He looked shocked.

"Are you sure, Mr J? What if it is King Brazi trying to fool us?" Maddie questioned, folding her arms.

"Yes, I thought the same, young Maddie. But I have spoken to them, and they assured me they sent the brooch," he explained. "They have been trying to find an easier way to get us to Rainbow Slide Park, but right now this is the best way. I trust them."

The group decided to stop for a breather. They needed it after working hard cleaning up.

"Is everyone hungry? I can call the kakaroonis to bring us some food," Dhow suggested.

"Yes, I am," Maddie said.

Theo offered them all a magical sweet to keep them going. He remembered Green Wonky Eyes from Head Office telling him the sweets would perk up the team members.

The unicwhales used a special noise to attract the kakaroonis. And quite often, right before lunchtime, a lot of the kakaroonis wandered the beautiful flower gardens. So, Dhow knew there would be some of them about. They loved to get out into nature and have a little walk. Dhow twisted her horn and clenched her teeth. It resembled a loud whistling noise, but it seemed to twirl through the air, not quite like an ordinary whistle. It spun about like an old-fashioned spinning top.

Within a few moments, kakaroonis surrounded them just outside the broken ride. It amazed Maddie and Theo how they had arrived with such speed. The kakaroonis knew the noise meant to bring food, so they arrived with special kakarooni food. Maddie, Theo, and Mr J turned their noses up. They didn't want to eat that sparkly stuff. The unicwhales and the kakaroonis all burst into laughter.

"Don't be daft. We wouldn't expect you to eat this. Even unicwhales don't eat kakarooni food. Theo, where is your bag?" Artcru asked him. She was still laughing, as were the others.

He pointed to his satchel. It was on the seat beside him.

He passed it over to Artcru, wondering what she was going to do. She opened the bag and pulled out a bubble wand. She stared at it for a moment but soon discarded it, throwing it onto the seat. Maddie grabbed it with delight in her eyes. Artcru threw her a look that said, *now is not the time, Maddie*, so she took the hint and placed it back on the seat. Artcru delved into the satchel once again and pulled out a small bottle of what looked like medicine.

"Aha, this is what I was looking for," she exclaimed, eyeing the liquid. It was about the size of a standard medicine bottle. She rummaged back inside the bag and pulled out a small spoon. She knew Head Office would have thought of everything. As she began to pour the liquid out of the bottle, Theo watched with fascination. It came out a bright green colour.

One of the kakaroonis leaned forward and passed Artcru a small plastic bowl filled with kakarooni biscuits. Artcru took the bowl and sprinkled a spoonful of medicine over the food. Then, she did the same over a second bowl. Maddie and Theo stared at the biscuits. They dissolved in front of their eyes. The biscuits fizzed and hissed and popped, and before long the bowl was empty. Maddie screwed her face up in disappointment, but Artcru watched her and said, "Just be patient."

Maddie crossed her arms and huffed.

Although the bowl was empty, the fizzing, popping, and hissing continued. After a few minutes, Maddie and Theo saw something begin to appear. It looked like pasta and vegetables. This was one of Theo's favourite dishes. He loved pasta. Artcru sprinkled some more magic medicine onto the pasta, and within seconds it turned into a yummy tomato- and chilli-flavoured sauce.

"Wow, this is amazing!" Maddie said. Theo couldn't speak. He was too amazed by it all. Mr J realised they only had one spoon between them all to eat with. He laughed at this but said nothing. He was happy to see what they did to resolve this.

They enjoyed their pasta meal. It was delicious. Theo and Maddie were more than happy sharing the spoon. Once they finished the first bowl together, the kakaroonis and Artcru produced a second bowl for the rest of them to share. Mr J didn't eat very much, being a small Jamaican owl, and neither did the unicwhales. They had small appetites. But they all felt full and satisfied. The kakaroonis headed off as it was time for their feed at the Cold Library.

"Thank you for sharing your food. It was so lovely," Theo said, hugging one of the kakaroonis before they left.

"Yes, it was so kind. Thank you," Maddie added.

• • •

"I wonder why Head Office didn't simply tell us where the secret passage was?" Maddie said to Theo as they walked. He shrugged his shoulders.

"I don't know," he replied.

"It is because they aren't always visible," Dhow explained. She was walking next to Maddie. "So, if Head Office had a look on the camera, they might not be able to see them. That and the fact that the secret passages change all the time."

Time was ticking along. They still had a good twenty-four hours and a bit, but they wanted to rescue the kakarooni as soon as possible.

They followed the instructions from the note and found the place where they thought the passage should be. The flower garden had taken a twist. That much was obvious. They walked along and had counted ten willow trees when the river ended abruptly. It veered off to the right and turned into a huge waterfall. It was beautiful. Straight ahead, the garden narrowed off. They all had to walk through a hedged archway, and before them was another dazzling flower garden. Through the other side of the arch they found a cobbled pathway, and to each side there were flower beds rife with pink roses, yellow carnations, heather, lavender, and plenty of other shrubs and flowers.

"Ouch, this brooch is really pinching me," Mincha moaned as she yanked it off her blue unicwhale skin.

"I can wear it if you want a break," Theo offered.

"Yes, please. At least you wear those human clothing things, so it won't pinch you." She passed the brooch over to him.

As they reached the pathway, Theo noticed it was only a short road. At the end of the pathway, he could see a round, enticing pond with a fountain in the middle. It was laced with a green hedgerow and dark purple acer trees. The fountain looked refreshing as it trickled into the pond. As they neared the pond, a small finch hopped into view, flapping his little wings.

"Aww, hello, little birdie. You look happy," Maddie said to him. He was tweeting away on the edge of the fountain. He seemed to be having a little wash. It was adorable to watch. She moved towards him, but he edged away. She couldn't quite reach him.

The group members decided to each head off on their own and have a look around to see if anything looked like a secret passage. If anyone found anything, they were to inform the others. It wasn't a massive area to search, but they thought it would save a little bit of time.

Maddie was the first to shout. She hailed them all over to the place she was investigating. She found a very small doorway hidden at the bottom of a tree. The tree grew in the middle of some laurel bushes.

"I don't think this is a secret passage. It's way too small for you lot to get through," Mr J said. "What do you think, unicwhales?" He lifted his head to look at them.

"It looks like a fairy home," Artcu said. Dhow and Mincha nodded.

"Yep, definitely a fairy home. These doorways are not secret passages." Dhow agreed.

The others sighed, and they each made their way back to the places they were searching.

It wasn't very long until they heard the next person make a noise. However, this time it was a scream.

It came from Theo's direction. It was a very loud scream. They ran over as the scream faded into the afternoon air.

Maddie was the first to reach Theo. She tried desperately to grab him, but she was too far away.

"Maddie..." he wailed as he spun and twisted into a black hole.

CHAPTER 6

Secret Passages and Dwarf Rabbits

Theo zoomed through the secret passage. It was like a dark tunnel, but it was fast and short. The experience was similar to a water slide, the only difference being the darkness and the lack of water. Theo couldn't see anything at all, and he didn't have a clue how long the tunnel would last. It was a tight space, and he was very glad when it came to an end. His hair was all stuck to his face. His face dripped with sweat, a product of his anxious thinking which kicked in as soon as he was sucked into the watering can. He couldn't understand how he had been sucked in when his whole body was so much larger than the watering can. It was impossible.

Fear washed over Theo as the tunnel came to an abrupt end. He popped out and landed on a bed of gravel. He almost toppled over from the force of the landing, but he managed to ground himself. It took a few minutes for his eyes to adjust. He had them closed tight in the tunnel and had crossed his arms over his body to protect himself. A few moments later his cap appeared at the end of the tunnel. He had lost it from the force. He grabbed it and placed it back on his head as he wiped the sweat from his face with the back of his arm.

Once Theo collected himself, he looked around. In front of him, he saw a wooden doorway. He moved towards it. It appeared quite small, but as he approached the door, he realised it was in fact full-sized. It had a round brass knob. Theo reached forward with both his hands and took it in his grip, but as he turned it, he realised it was locked. He was trapped.

He sat on the floor in a dark corner. It was a little cold and damp. He guessed he was inside a tree trunk. He curled up with his knees bent, his feet flat on the floor, and his arms tucked around them to keep himself warm. He was trying to think without getting too overwhelmed. He was sure Maddie and the others would be working on a way to rescue him or get to him somehow. He would have to sit tight.

It was a small area that he was trapped in, and there wasn't a massive amount of room to move about. The ceiling was high enough for him to stand up straight. Although it was dark, he could just make out that it was about the size of an under-stairs cupboard. He hoped there weren't any spiders as he was petrified by them. His thoughts began to wander off. He wondered who locked him in here. His first guess was either the kidnapper or King Brazi. It stood to reason.

He felt a little tired, so he closed his eyes and nodded off. He was woken by a strange noise. It took him a minute to remember where he was. The noise came from the corner opposite him.

He scrambled up onto his feet, trying to be quiet. He didn't want to be attacked by whatever was making the noise. He wanted to be poised and ready. He could almost make out a small creature. It looked a little bit like a rabbit, but it was much smaller and stockier. He wore dungarees, and a carrot dangled from his mouth. Theo could almost hear him say, "What's up, doc?"

The dwarf rabbit stopped whatever he was doing. Theo couldn't quite make out what that was. He looked over at Theo, released the carrot from his mouth, and said, "Ah, boy, you are awake. Pleased to meet you. I am Mr Rabwarf. Come and help me. I am trying to get us out of here."

Theo moved with caution over to Mr Rabwarf. He could see now that the rabbit had been hammering away at the inside of the tree.

"Look at this teeny-weeny hole here. I am trying to make it bigger so we can escape." He pulled Theo closer to the bark.

"Oh, yes, I will help you." Theo looked around. Although it was dark, he caught a glimpse of a small cluster of rocks on the floor in the corner. Grabbing the biggest of the bunch, he began to help Rabwarf chip away at the bark wall.

"My name is Theo. How did you get in here?" Theo asked him. He was intrigued because it looked like there was no way in or out except through the secret passage, which had since disappeared.

"I work for Head Office. I fell down a hole, and it seems I ended up here." Mr Rabwarf didn't seem fazed.

"There are lots of random hidden passages dotted about in this zoo, you know," he explained to Theo. "I often come to help when things get a bit tricky in the zoo for novices in Imagination World. So, I decided that since I am here, I may as well help you, boy. After all, I know the zoo pretty well."

So, the pair of them got to work hammering away in hopes of escaping the tree.

They hadn't been hammering for very long when Mr Rabwarf and Theo heard a rumble. They were making progress, but it was slow. The noise came from the same tunnel that brought Theo. They turned to see what all the commotion was about and saw the tunnel had reappeared.

CHAPTER 7

More Secret Passages and Finches

"Oh no! He's gone," Maddie shouted as the others approached. "The watering can sucked him in. What are we going to do, Mr J?" Her heart thudded in her chest, and her hands felt clammy.

This was not supposed to happen. But he was wearing the brooch. Theo had gone, and they were all left behind.

"He was looking inside," she explained. "He bent right down, and as soon as I reached him, he got sucked in. He just disappeared." They each had a look inside to see if there was any trace of him left. No one feared being sucked in because they knew it would only work if they wore the brooch. Seeing no trace of Theo, they were left wondering what to do.

"I thought we all had to hold hands to go through," Maddie said. She was so shocked he had been sucked in on his own.

"Well, the note did say that whoever wears it would go first," Mincha said, reminding her. "Others can go if they are all holding hands, but it didn't say we would all definitely be going together."

Mr J was not a happy owl. Things seemed to be getting worse. Now they had a kidnapped kakarooni and a lost Theo.

"Any of you clever unicwhales happen to know where the secret passage leads to?" Mr J asked. "We'll have to go on a hunt now to find Theo. If anyone has any bright ideas, it would be great to hear them."

"It goes straight to the helter-skelter," Mincha said.

"No, it doesn't. It goes to the magical mirrors."

"No, Artcu, it goes to the helter-skelter. I know these passages best. Dhow, tell him. I am right." Mincha crossed her arms and pursed her lips.

"I don't have a clue, but let's not argue. It won't help," Dhow said.

So, they were none the wiser. This knocked them all a bit, and the atmosphere amongst the remaining five was miserable, to say the least. They messed up, and now it had cost them Theo. Maddie noticed a bench opposite where they stood, and she made her way towards it. She needed a moment to think. The others followed. Mincha felt thirsty, so she toddled off to the food stand. She brought back some bottles of water for each of them. It turned out warm and sunny as the day progressed, so keeping up their hydration was important.

"I have an idea, Mr J. Why don't we try and follow Theo down the watering can?" Maddie couldn't see what harm it could do.

"Well, we can try, I suppose. We don't have anything to lose. And I hate calling Head Office all the time, especially as we didn't follow their instructions. I think they will be mad with me."

"Come on then." Maddie jumped off the bench and marched over to the watering can. She stared into the nozzle and shouted for Theo. Nothing happened. Mr J flew over and landed on the rim.

"Maybe if you hold onto me and I jump in?" He raised his eyebrows.

"Yes, let's try it. Are you three going to come too? Dhow, you hold onto me, and you two hold onto Dhow." Maddie instructed, pointing to Artcru and Mincha.

Mr J was balanced on the side, ready to take the plunge. They all stood still with their eyes closed as he jumped in. Maddie felt a tug on her arm, but when she opened her eyes, nothing had happened. Mr J was inside the can, and the rest of them were holding hands outside. She looked over at the unicwhales. They opened their eyes. Maddie clenched her teeth. She could see the others looked fed up and frustrated too.

"Mr J, are you okay?" Maddie peered into the watering can. She could see him tucked up into the corner.

"I am fine. I guess that didn't work. Can you help me out, please, my dear?" he asked.

Maddie's arm was still inside the can, so she pulled him out and set him on the ground. She sat down next to him on the cold floor, crossed her legs, cupped her head in her hands, and stared at him.

"Now what?" she asked.

Mr J was out of ideas. They sat deep in thought for a few moments. Then, Maddie jumped to her feet.

"Oooh, I have an idea," she announced. "Wait there." Without another word, she sprung away towards the pond.

"Hey, mister. Can you help me with something?" She asked the little finch. She was happy to see he was still there.

He had finished his bath, but he was still playing about in the water. The finch stopped what he was doing. His head bobbed up, and he stared directly at Maddie. He edged away a little.

"Don't be scared. I won't hurt you. I only want your help. My friend got sucked down the watering can, and now we need to follow him. But it seems to have closed up." She moved closer to him. "Do you know anything about the secret passages around here?"

"I don't know anything. I can't help you. I'm sorry. Please leave me alone," he squeaked. He sounded more like a mouse than a bird. She thought he was so cute.

"Please, Mr Bird. We need to find the kidnapper." She grinned as she clasped her hands together in a praying motion.

"Look, if I help you, Brazi will come after me. He has eyes everywhere," he explained, edging further away from Maddie. But she followed and moved in closer still.

"He isn't here. He won't know you have helped. Please, please help us. I promise I won't tell anyone you said anything. No one will know." Maddie begged and pleaded. "Don't you want us to save the kakarooni? I will do something to help you. What can I do?"

The finch didn't move away this time but stayed quiet for a few moments. Maddie waited.

"I will tell you one thing, and then please go and don't ask me anything else," he whispered, his little eyes darting about.

"Thank you, thank you. I promise," Maddie replied.

"There is another watering can in this garden. It will take you to the same place as Theo. But there is a secret code word you need to get through it. I can't tell you that. Now go." He flapped his wings, preparing to fly away.

Maddie leant over and kissed him. She felt a desperate urge to ask what the code word was or where to find it, but she resisted pushing him. She ran back over to the others as he flew away.

They all seemed happy enough to search for another watering can. It wasn't a huge area. Maddie thought they didn't have too many other options anyway. They all agreed that keeping Head Office out of this issue seemed sensible.

Mr J, Mincha, and Artcru sauntered off towards the other side of the pond while Maddie and Dhow searched around their area. As they hunted, Maddie remembered the yellow poppies and asked Dhow about them.

"Okay, I will do my best to explain. The yellow poppies are magical, Maddie. However, they come with a twist—a bit like the brooch, I guess. There are always conditions and consequences where magic is concerned. At least that is how it works here in Kakarooni Zoo."

Maddie's eyes were wide with excitement. She loved learning new things. Something as exciting as magic had her hooked.

"What is the twist?" she asked, her eyes twinkling in the sunshine. She moved forward to concentrate on every word Dhow told her.

"Well, Maddie, the yellow poppies are a portal. A portal is like a secret passage. It transports you to some other place. So, in the case of these poppies, they will transport you out of Imagination World." Maddie inched forward again.

"So, this is why you must never touch them," Dhow continued. "For some reason, you were lucky the other day; I think maybe I caught you just in time. If you had rubbed the poppy for much longer, you would have been gone."

"Oh, I see. I didn't realise," Maddie said. It made more sense now.

"And then, of course, there is the twist. It might not seem like a big deal if you were to leave Imagination World via the yellow poppies. However, you cannot return until at least twenty-four hours have passed."

"So, if we need to get home, is that how we do it?" she asked. Dhow confirmed this. It was the only way to leave Imagination World.

Before they could continue, they were interrupted by a loud shout. Well, more of a squawk. Mr J had found the watering can.

Maddie, Mr J, and the unicwhales gathered round it. Maddie chewed at her nails. She wanted this to work. She felt bad that Theo was all on his own. She knew he wasn't very brave at the best of times, but in a strange world all by himself, she was sure he would be scared and anxious.

They all stood outside the watering can. As there was no brooch this time and they weren't too sure what to do, Dhow suggested they at least hold hands.

Maddie explained what the finch told her, but none of them had a clue how to figure out the secret code.

"So, what do we do think the secret code word is going to be?" Artcru asked.

"We simply need to keep trying things," Mr J said.

"I think we should try something simple, like open sesame," Mincha said. Maddie liked this idea, although she wondered if that was too simple. Yet it had worked with the magic wand, and they had nothing to lose.

"Are we all ready, then?" Mr J asked. Maddie held him tight in her hand, ready to balance him on the edge and then take hold of his wing. They all felt a little nervous, but they were also excited. Maddie wondered what to expect of the secret passageway.

Mr J took a long, deep breath in and jumped as he shouted the words. "Open sesame." They closed their eyes and waited.

After a few seconds, Maddie realised everything felt the same. She opened one eye to peek about. Realising nothing had happened, she opened the other eye.

"Oh, now what?" She sighed. She could feel the tension in Dhow's hand.

They decided to try again, but still, nothing happened. Maddie tightened her mouth and frowned. *There has to be a way to get through these passages,* she thought to herself.

"I have an idea," Artcru said. "Maybe Mincha needs to say the words. After all, she found the brooch in the first place, so maybe that is the twist here. There is nearly always a twist with magic, as we know."

It was a good idea and well worth a shot. Maddie gripped Mr J tighter. Her whole body felt tense, and she felt it in his small frame too.

They all had their eyes closed. Maddie felt a sudden suction. Her body felt like it had been squeezed to fit through a small, tight hole. Within seconds they whooshed through the tunnel. It all happened so quickly. They seemed to shrivel up one by one and shrink into nothingness. Maddie peeked and noticed a puff of colourful smoke, and a split second later they entered the tunnel.

The journey through the tunnel was an amazing experience for Maddie. She loved every second, although it didn't last for very long. It was similar to a water slide, but for Maddie and the others it wasn't dark. This tunnel was colourful. Many coloured squares made up the tunnel—pinks, blues, greens, and yellows. Arrows on the sides pointed downwards. All they could see in front of them was a black hole right at the bottom. It looked like it would go on forever, and Maddie feared they would never reach it.

However, it wasn't long before they were spat out at the bottom, landing on their feet. They all toppled over from the force and speed of the tunnel. And, of course, they were all still holding hands. They landed on each other, causing one large pileup. In front of them, Maddie saw Theo.

She jumped up, untangled herself from the others, and ran over to hug him. She had a huge grin on her face.

"What is this place? Where are we?" she asked him.

CHAPTER 8

Adninjas and Helter-Skelters

Theo couldn't believe his eyes: it was Maddie and the rest of the group. They made it; they found him. He was so happy. It had been lovely getting to know Mr Rabwarf a little bit, and it was nice to have a friend. But he sure missed his tribe. His grin spread from ear to ear. Maddie ran up to him and gave him the biggest hug.

"Yippee!" she screeched. "We found you, Theo." Theo seemed equally pleased to see her as well. He had missed her.

It was cosy in here now with all these extra bodies. It had been snug enough beforehand, and the unicwhales weren't the smallest of creatures.

"Hi, guys. I'm Mr Rabwarf." He stepped forward to greet them all. "Hey, Mr J. It's been a while, mate. How are you, old pal?" he asked politely.

"Rabwarf, I am doing well, thanks. I'm grateful I have these guys helping me. It's a tough quest."

For a few minutes, they all exchanged pleasantries and hugs. They swapped stories. Mr Rabwarf informed them that they were at the helter-skelter area, trapped inside this tree.

"I don't understand why Head Office told me you were at Rainbow Slide Park. I wonder what they are playing at." Mr J pondered. "Did Head Office send you here?" he asked Rabwarf.

"Nope, I fell in here by mistake," he replied. He looked bewildered.

"Something doesn't seem to quite add up here. But anyway, here we are," Mr J said.

Theo complained that he felt thirsty. He had already disappeared before Mincha bought them all water.

"Check your satchel," Rabwarf suggested. "There may be water." Theo opened the flap and pulled everything out. He was surprised to find a small bottle of water right at the bottom. Taking a huge gulp, he felt satisfied in an instant. He drank more, enjoying the feeling.

Between them, they decided to keep on chipping away at the hole in the tree for now. It seemed the best course of action.

"I hope the kidnapper hasn't got too far ahead of us," Mr J said. "As soon as we get out of this tree, we need to get to Rainbow Slide Park. I'm not too sure how far away we are from it though." Theo thought he looked a little haggard.

"Guys, if we are at the helter-skelter area, I reckon we will be able to find another secret passage. It's coming back to me how to spot them," Dhow said.

It wasn't long before they created a hole large enough to clamber through. It wasn't huge, but they managed to squeeze their bodies through it. Maddie and Theo had no trouble. However, the unicwhales needed more of a helping hand. Mr J and Mr Rabwarf followed with little fuss.

It was still light outside. Theo and Mr Rabwarf had been trapped inside the dark tree for a while, so the light hit them hard. Theo blinked and squinted. They all crept out slow but steady as they figured out their bearings. The helter-skelter awaited them directly to their right. It was so huge that they couldn't miss it. But the last time Theo, Maddie, and Mr J were there, the sun had already set. It looked different in the daylight—more inviting.

There were a lot of children playing on the slide. Maddie and Theo thought it looked great and wished they could have a go on it.

"We need you two to have a go on the slide," Rabwarf told the children. "Mr J and I think it would be sensible to check for adninjas. So, if you go on the helter-skelter, you can check that area out while we have a nose about down and around here for the kidnapper and kakarooni. Okay?"

Theo and Maddie nodded.

"What should we do if we see them?" Theo asked. He tucked his hands into his pockets, then turned his head and took a quick sideways glance at Mr J.

"You are more likely to feel them than see them. Holler if this happens. Otherwise, we'll see you in a few minutes. Enjoy the ride," Rabwarf said, pushing them towards the helter-skelter. "The unicwhales are going for a rest. Meet us over there when you have finished." He pointed to a large family picnic area on the other side of the helter-skelter.

"Come on, Theo. I can't wait to have a go on the helter-skelter. I love these slides." Maddie grabbed his hand. As soon as Mr J and Rabwarf made the suggestion, Maddie and Theo dashed away to the ride. There was a queue and a lot of steps to climb, but that didn't put them off at all. In fact, they ran up the steps two at a time.

As they waited near the top, Theo turned to Maddie. "I'm having the best time in Imagination World. Are you? I'm so glad you made me stick around at the railway station. I was pretty scared, trapped inside the tree, although it was better when Mr Rabwarf turned up."

"Yes, Theo, I agree. I am having the best time, too. I really hope we can outsmart this kidnapper, though, and rescue the kakarooni. That would be the best end to all of this. But I do love all the fun things we are getting to do. I love Mr J as well. He is the best Jamaican owl ever!"

"Argh!" Theo screamed. He giggled at the same time, and he could hear Maddie making lots of happy noises, too. She was directly below him. Many times he caught a glimpse of her, and just as he thought he would catch up, she zoomed off round the next twisty corner.

"That was so cool, Theo." Maddie was jumping up and down as Theo skidded to a halt, his hair flapping away under his cap.

"This is my favourite by far," Theo said.

"Me, too!" Maddie said. "Come on. We should go back to the others." They made their way over to the unicwhales hand in hand, skipping and laughing.

Mr J and Mr Rabwarf sat with them.

"You had fun, then, you pair?" Mr J asked.

"It was the best, Mr J, thank you. But there were no adninjas," said Theo. He felt warm and a little breathless.

"So, what is happening, then? Any news on the kidnapper?" Maddie asked.

Mr J shook his head. While Maddie and Theo rode the helter-skelter, Mr J and Rabwarf had spent their time wandering about and asking people if they had seen the kidnapper.

"Of course, we had to ask if they saw a man who could transform himself. We had some strange looks, that's for sure. It was bad enough being a talking owl and a dwarf rabbit. We only asked children." Mr J laughed at himself.

"I bet it was funny to see those children's faces when you asked them those silly questions," Theo said, laughing along with Mr J.

"Yes, one child told us she saw the kakarooni tied up earlier on. There was a man with him. But he wasn't there for long. She watched him go over and lock the door on the tree, and then he disappeared."

"But where did the kakarooni go when he disappeared?" Maddie asked.

"The kakarooni was still tied up, but another kakarooni came along and stayed with him for a while. Then she left to play on the helter-skelter, and when she reached the bottom, they were gone," Mr J finished.

"Well, surely the other kakarooni was the kidnapper, Mr J?" Theo questioned.

"Yes, I would have thought so," he said in agreement.

"So, we have missed him again," Maddie said. She sighed.

"Oh, hang on. She also said she thought she saw the man leave something over by the tree when he locked the door. Let's go take a look, kids."

Mr J was sure it was the kidnapper. Theo, Maddie, and the Jamaican owl made their way back to the tree. One branch of the tree hung low, and a small glass jar dangled from a piece of string tied around the end. Tucked inside the jar was a folded piece of paper. Maddie stretched up onto her tiptoes, reached her hand inside the jar, and retrieved the paper.

Mr J read it out loud. "*You have missed me again, fools! I was here, but I was smart enough to trap you inside the tree. I knew you would figure a way out soon enough. See you at Rainbow Slide Park. If you think you can catch up with me.*"

Theo burned with fury. They were so close. If only he hadn't fallen through the watering can, they would have all been here together. They could have gotten out quicker and fought off the kidnapper. Once again, they were a few steps behind.

The three returned to the unicwhales and Mr Rabwarf feeling defeated. Maddie had a cuddle with Mincha, which seemed to make her feel a little better. Mr Rabwarf stood up, sniffed the air, and said, "It's not all doom and gloom, you know. There is a very quick way out of here that takes you straight to Rainbow Slide Park."

CHAPTER 9

Rainbow Slide Park

Mr Rabwarf led them back to the helter-skelter. It was quiet now. Most of the children had gone to other parts of the zoo, and Maddie saw a few over on the go-karts and teacups. One or two still climbed the steps, hungry for the thrill of the awesome twisty slide.

"You need to feel around for a secret pocket inside your sack," Rabwarf explained to the children. "You might not find it straight away because they will be in different places in each sack. So, it might take a couple of goes." Maddie and Theo were happy to have extra goes, that was for sure.

Maddie loved a helter-skelter, partly because it was the only slide where she had ever ridden tucked inside a hairy hessian sack.

Mr Rabwarf gave them each a £1 coin and instructed them to insert the coin when they found their secret pocket. He couldn't tell them what would happen next because it was always a different outcome. He only knew this was the fastest way to get to Rainbow Slide Park.

They climbed up the steps inside the twisty tower. Once they reached the top, the man at the controls gave them all a sack, and off they went one by one down the helter-skelter.

• • •

Maddie was the first down the helter-skelter, and following Mr Rabwarf's instructions, she found her secret pocket straight away. She inserted the £1 coin, and within seconds the sack catapulted into the air. Everything went blurry, and she heard a fizzing noise all around her. She wondered if the others saw it happen or if anyone else in the zoo saw them flying through the air. The next few seconds she couldn't account for. It all turned black, and the next thing she knew she was bouncing onto this water slide.

Maddie landed first, diving into Rainbow Slide Park. She found herself on a long, colourful, bumpy slide. Her sack had turned into a rubber ring, and her legs dangled over the side. She spun all over the place, and when she could see forward, it looked as though she was headed for a pool of water at the bottom of the slide. But the water wasn't ordinary; it was rainbow-coloured with glitter running through it.

Maddie screamed with delight into the open air. "This is so much fun!" she cried.

The slide was quite wide, wide enough for the rubber ring, and another slide ran alongside hers. The slide was made up of coloured zigzag lines—pink, blue, green, purple, and orange. It dazzled with brightness, but it was very beautiful at the same time.

Maddie zipped toward the water at a very fast pace indeed, and her heart began to flutter. She didn't want it to end.

She noticed Theo on the slide to her left. They both sped down the slide at the same rapid pace.

"Wowzers, that was so much fun. Did you love it, Theo?" she asked him as they both hit the bottom. The water was a few inches deep at most, so they only got a light splashing. Maddie climbed out of her ring and ran over to him.

Theo's grin was wider than she had ever seen it before. "Yes, it was great fun. I love water slides."

"Look, there's Mr Rabwarf and Mr J." Maddie pointed at the two, laughing her head off. Mr J looked so small in the huge rubber ring.

He held on by his little Jamaican beak. Each side of the ring had a grab handle, which he latched onto and held for dear life. It was hilarious to watch, but she doubted whether it was as funny for him experiencing it. Maddie imagined he was quite frightened. Mr Rabwarf, although a fair amount bigger than Mr J, was also quite small to be inside one of these huge rings. They both made some rather strange noises as they hurtled towards Maddie and Theo.

The unicwhales weren't far behind. They looked as if they were chilling and enjoying the ride. Once they were all together at the bottom of the slide, Mr J had gotten back to his usual bird-like self. Although, he did look a little green from the ride, which clashed with his bright pink streak.

"It finally feels like we are getting somewhere now," Maddie said. "I am so happy we have made it to Rainbow Slide Park. Woohoo, guys! High five." Her smile said it all. She smacked her hand against Theo's. He too was smiling. His face beamed.

Although it wasn't possible to see the whole park from ground level, Maddie and Theo were amazed by its beauty and colour. It looked like such a well-designed, magical place. They were super keen to get exploring here. The colours were so vibrant and bold. Everything sparkled and glittered in the sunshine. Even the birds and trees were colourful.

"Can we have another quick go on the slide, Mr J?" Maddie asked.

"Of course not. We must get on. Come along," Mr J said, marching off. Maddie knew better than to whine, but she looked over at Theo and pulled a silly face. He giggled at her.

At the bottom of the water slide, nine pathways led off in different directions. The whole park looked like a giant octopus with an extra tentacle. Each path was long and striped with colours—pinks, blues, yellows, greens. At the end of each pathway was another slide. All nine slides looked different from one another. Some were water slides, and some not. In between each pathway and slide area, there were beautiful flower gardens. Again, each flower garden was different. There was a toilet block located to the left and a food block to the right. Houses lined the edges of the park. Rabwarf pointed at the houses.

"Those homes belong to the unicwhales. This is where they come from," he told the children.

The park was huge, and everything in it seemed double its normal size. It was simple enough, though, and consisted of those few things: slides, flower gardens, and the unicwhale homes. Maddie hoped they would be able to get around the whole park and try out each slide at least once.

Theo turned to Maddie with utter disbelief on his face. "Wow, Maddie, can this zoo get any better? I would love to visit the unicwhale homes. They look unusual, totally different from the kakarooni cages."

"I know. It is such a great place, isn't it? I do hope we can come back another day to play here." Maddie would have loved to visit the unicwhale homes too.

As they walked, Mr J received a call from Head Office.

After Mr J ended the call, Theo asked, "Why did Head Office lie to you, Mr J? Why didn't they tell you where I was?"

"They didn't want me or anyone else to panic. They thought that if we all believed we were going straight to you and Rainbow Slide Park, then we wouldn't worry or ask questions."

"That seems a bit strange. I don't understand why adults lie," Maddie said.

"Well, sometimes they do what they think is most helpful. They thought we would deal with what faced us once we reached Theo," Mr J explained.

"They said the kidnapper is in Rainbow Slide Park now, for sure," he continued. "They saw him on camera. He forgot about his superpower for a moment, it seems, and he revealed himself. He was last seen over by the food block in a flower garden. So, lovely children, Mr Rabwarf, and you crazy unicwhales, let's get moving. Shall we?" Mr J said. He seemed to be back to his jolly self since calling Head Office. Things were back on track.

• • •

It was a good stroll from the centre of Rainbow Slide Park to the flower garden near the food block. Maddie realised the park was symmetrical, so she now knew how long it would take them to get anywhere within the park.

She was glad they were near the food block as well—what a bonus. A couple of hours had passed since she had begun to feel a little peckish, and now her belly rumbled violently. Back at home, her aunt made their dinner on the dot at six p.m. She wasn't sure of the time, but she knew by her tummy that it had to be around six.

Mr Rabwarf emptied his pockets. Along with the usual pocket fluff, he pulled out a few spare coins. He treated them to a nice round of burgers and chips. The unicwhales and Mr J (who all ate small portions) shared a couple of sausages and some chips.

"Do you have special food like the kakaroonis?" Maddie asked Mincha.

"Yes, but it isn't the nicest tasting. We prefer human food," Mincha explained.

Once they were all full and satisfied, they crossed the colourful pathway and made their way into the gorgeous flower gardens.

"Wow, look at all these beautiful flowers. I love tulips." Maddie pointed to the red, yellow, and white flowers blossoming in front of them. "Mmm, they smell so good too." She pinched one of the stems and sunk her nose into the petals.

As the smell hit the back of her nose, it reminded her of the yellow roses back home. She was taken back to her garden, and for a brief second she felt homesick.

Theo joined her, taking in the gorgeous smells. "They are pretty, Maddie. I like flowers too. My favourite are daisies. Mum always has some in our garden."

Another pathway led them down to a pond. However, this pond wasn't circular. Rather, it zigzagged all around the garden. In it were a couple of fountains and stepping stones leading across to the other side. Over the other side, Maddie saw a patch of crocuses—purple, white, and yellow ones all mixed together. She also spotted a magnolia tree in full bloom. She loved magnolias. There was one in the corner of her aunt's back garden at home.

Flower beds dotted all about the garden, intermixed with squares of lush green grass. A few benches lined the water's edge, allowing a nice, peaceful place to watch and listen to the crystal-clear pond. In the distance, Maddie heard the hum of a lawnmower. They kept the gardens neat and tidy here. Out of the corner of her eye, she noticed a very small cottage in the distance, hidden from view behind some large cherry trees.

"Look, Theo. There's a cottage. I wonder who lives in it." She pointed across. "I want to go and see." Theo followed her gaze.

Before he had a chance to answer, Mr J and the others were beside them.

"Right then, here is the plan of action," Mr J said. "If you all agree, I think we should begin looking around for the kidnapper and the kakarooni. Like before, we'll each take an area. It will be a difficult task because of his superpower. So, let's work together. Quick and smart."

. . .

Maddie, Theo, and Mr J decided they would venture across the stepping stones and begin the search over that side of the flower garden. It meant they were all spread out a little bit. It was a large garden, and there was a lot of area to cover.

Mincha and Artcru decided to search together while Dhow and Mr Rabwarf teamed up. There weren't many people about now as it was almost closing time at the zoo. But they were all mindful that the kidnapper could be any one of the few people they saw, or he could be disguised as anything. They hoped that having the kakarooni with him would somehow make him a little easier to spot.

As they crossed the pond, they looked into the water to see if he had somehow hidden himself in the depths, but it was crystal clear, and they saw nothing. So, unless he had turned himself into a frog or some other water-living creature, they decided he wasn't hiding in there. Maddie almost toppled into the pond as she leant forward but caught herself just in time.

"Do you think he could be disguised as a flower, Mr J?" Maddie asked him. She left nothing uninvestigated. She checked every single flower bed to see if he had morphed into anything.

"Or he could have tied the kakarooni up somewhere, and now he's hiding as something," she continued.

"Yes, young Maddie, he could be anywhere. It is all possible. We simply need to keep looking everywhere we can think of," Mr J answered.

She continued to look upwards in case he was in a tree. There weren't that many places to hide because everything was outside and in the open. It sure seemed like a difficult task.

Many bushes and hedges edged the garden on both sides, separating it from the colourful pathways. Theo scrambled through hedge after hedge to no avail. It wasn't long until he got fed up and frustrated.

"Maddie," he shouted over to her, "I'm getting nowhere. This is a silly task. We are never going to find him."

Maddie strolled over to Theo and did what she did best. She gave him a nice warm hug. He looked so sad. His eyes were narrow, but he lowered his head and snuggled into her shoulder. She could understand his frustration. They needed a new idea or a clue or something.

"Come on, let's go and see Mr J. It will all be okay." They made their way over to Mr J and told him their concerns. But as he was about to respond, Dhow shouted from across the river.

"Guys, you need to come over here quickly. I think I know where we can find him."

Dhow had found a maze right at the back of the garden. Well, she had seen lots of hedges that all looked higgledy-piggledy. So, she only assumed it was some kind of maze. *What a great place to go and hide if you were on the run,* Maddie thought.

They all agreed it was a brilliant idea to go and have a look. They had nothing to lose.

The maze was huge, and the hedges were so tall. Even the unicwhales couldn't see over them. They spotted a gap, which formed the entrance, and made their way through with Dhow taking the lead.

"Dhow, if you are from this park, how come you didn't know about the maze?" Maddie asked her, intrigued.

"Good question. The park changes sometimes. Things don't always stay the same." She thought for a moment. "Some areas seem to do so, and some don't. So, you never know what you are going to find. But unicwhales know the zoo better than anyone as much as we can."

They walked straight ahead. There wasn't much straightness to the path, though. The maze took many twists and turns. It wasn't long before they realised they were lost. They all stuck together, working as a team. The last thing they wanted was to lose Theo again, or anyone else.

"I don't think there is anyone else in here. It's very quiet. Surely if the kidnapper was hiding here, we would come across him," Theo said as they came to yet another turning point. Maddie opted to go left, but none of them had any way of knowing what the best route was. They simply had to follow their noses.

"Yeah, the zoo is now closed. So, if we meet anyone, it will be him," Mr J said.

They continued their stroll, and Maddie hoped an exit to the other side wouldn't be too difficult to find. She glanced at the others, and their faces seemed to tell the same story. The gravel crunched beneath their feet. A chill formed in the air as the time passed from afternoon to early evening. The light had begun to fade. Maddie hoped they would find their way out before it got dark. She wasn't a fan of the dark, and she thought it would be even scarier in here amongst all the hedges.

"Oh, look. I think we have made it." Maddie pointed to what looked like the exit. The hedges came to an end, and there was a huge gap. They had reached a certain point, and from here the twists and turns stopped. It led out at the back of the gardens.

Maddie saw a pathway of large slate stepping stones placed amongst scattered bark. Traces of weeds peeked through the cracks. On either side of the pathway spread an array of colourful flowers, all the colours of the rainbow. She had never seen anything like it. The pathway ran through an unusual tunnel of heart-shaped arches. There were six small metal heart-shaped frames. Each one was covered in roses—the first one red roses, the second pink, the third one yellow. The next three followed the same pattern.

"Wow! Look at those hearts, Theo. Aren't they gorgeous?" Maddie said. "I'm going to run all the way through them to the other side."

She didn't wait for Theo or anyone else to say they were joining her. She pushed her hair out of her face and sprinted away, whooping with all the joys, freedom, and happiness of an eight-year-old. It didn't take her long to get to the end. She paused for breath, and on her return, she hopped and jumped onto each stepping stone, laughing as she went and making sure she didn't fall and step on any of the bark chippings.

Maddie rambled as she made it back to the others. "The little cottage I noticed earlier is right up there after you run through the hearts. Can we go and look at it? It looks so cute." She turned to Mr J, to whom she often directed her questions.

Mr J nodded. "Come on, then. We can search for the kidnapper while we are having a mooch around. Although there aren't many places left around this garden to search for him." With that, he toddled off under the heart arches, bouncing from steppingstone to steppingstone until he reached the top. The arches and the steps curved into a slight bend. The path seemed to incline too. The cottage was set at the top and could not be seen from the bottom.

As they passed a birdfeeder, Maddie noticed a little black-and-brown sparrow perched on the edge, pecking away at the food. He looked happy as he tweeted away. Maddie stopped to stroke the little fella, but he flew away before she could reach him. She noticed another small birdfeeder attached to the low-hanging roof of the cottage. She couldn't wait to see who lived there. She glanced up at the cottage. The windows were laced with honeysuckle. The house itself was made of wood—more of a cabin than a cottage. It looked tiny, much too small to be lived in. It only had one door and two windows. She wondered what it was like on the inside.

The unicwhales lagged behind, dragging themselves up the stepping stones. Mr J and Rabwarf waited at the top with Maddie and Theo. They had passed the birdfeeders, and now they were nosing all around the outside of the cottage. Theo noticed the door was ajar, so he gave it a push. As it opened, Maddie saw a man stretched out on the sofa. He appeared to be asleep. The others peered over Theo's shoulder. He lifted his finger to his lips and silently pulled the door shut. They moved away from the cottage, each wondering what to do. Silence fell over the group for a few moments.

Mr J spoke up first. "That is the kidnapper. I am sure of it." The owl kept his Jamaican-accented voice low. He didn't want to wake the man.

"What are we going to do? Where do you think the kakarooni is?" Maddie whispered. The place was not big enough for a kakarooni to be inside as well. There was only one room, and there was no kakarooni with the kidnapper.

"I think we need to go in and face him. Hopefully, it will scare him into releasing the kakarooni or at least telling us where he is keeping him," Mr Rabwarf said. He puffed out his chest and lifted his head high.

They all agreed they needed to face the kidnapper. It was no good being this close to him and not acting on it.

As Theo pushed the door open a second time, Maddie was shocked to see the kidnapper had disappeared. She couldn't believe her eyes. A few seconds ago he was asleep on the sofa. Now he was nowhere to be seen.

· · ·

They left the cottage after having had a good look around to see if they could spot the kidnapper.

"He must have heard us and used his superpower. He couldn't have escaped otherwise," Mr J said.

Mr Rabwarf offered a guess. "Yeah, he probably morphed into a tiny mouse. Then, he could easily squeeze through any small gap. We would never have noticed him."

There were no clues left inside the cottage that they could see, only half a cup of cold coffee on the side table and an open book lying face down beside it. They searched outside and around the back too. Theo found a chain that resembled a dog collar. He must have had the kakarooni tied up out there.

"They can't have gone far. It has only been a few minutes. I can't believe we didn't hear them." Theo looked puzzled.

Everyone agreed and decided to head back towards the hedged maze. There didn't seem to be another way to get back, so he must have gone that way. As they entered, Maddie looked up and thought it seemed different somehow. It was pretty dark now. The end of yet another day. Maddie wondered where they would sleep tonight.

"I think we should get through this maze as quickly as we can," Rabwarf said. "It ain't a nice place to be hanging around in the dark. It has definitely changed, and it moves constantly. We don't want to be getting lost." He confirmed Maddie's suspicions.

As they turned the next corner, Theo screamed. Maddie's whole body stiffened as she watched him come face to face with King Brazi. And he wasn't alone. He and his team of adninjas blocked the way.

"Well, well, well. Who have we here, then? If it isn't the tribe of do-gooders, themselves. Bet you thought you were onto something, catching up with the kidnapper like that, didn't you?" He laughed. His deep, throaty laugh disturbed Maddie's ears.

"Oh, go away, Brazi," Maddie screamed. "We have had enough of you and your silly adninjas. You don't scare us. Move!" She lunged forward as she spoke, almost head-butting him.

"No chance! You silly young girl," he spat back, swishing towards her as he continued to yell.

"As I keep trying to tell you, you will never catch him. He will always be a step ahead, especially with my help. So, come on, then. Do your best. If you want to get any further, let's fight." He scrunched his fist into a ball and lurched his hand up into the air.

The fight scene wasn't a pretty one. It began before they had time to think. The adninjas attacked, so they had no choice but to defend themselves. They played a lot dirtier than they had during the simple go-kart battle. Mr J and Rabwarf were getting a little battered and squashed. The dark, wispy creatures kicked, punched, and screeched into the air. They pulled branches off the hedges and swung them at the children and the unicwhales. Maddie and Theo were quite fast though. They ducked and dived and managed to avoid getting much more than a few scratches.

"Oww." Theo winced. One of their thrusts had cut his arm open. It wasn't too deep a cut, but the branch scratched him enough to make it bleed.

Maddie gasped. "Are you okay?"

"I'll manage," Theo shouted back. He rubbed the blood away as best he could with his other hand.

Maddie didn't understand how the adninjas were back. She thought they were dead and gone forever after the children killed them off in the go-kart battle. Yet they came back to life somehow. She wondered if they were ever going to be able to kill them off altogether.

"What do you want?" Maddie screeched at Brazi. "Leave us alone. We know where the kidnapper is, and we are going to get him."

Brazi laughed at her. He floated towards her as his adninjas continued to attack. His eyes looked evil as they drilled into her. He gritted his teeth, and with his wispy hand he grabbed her chin and held her face tight and still. His stale breath made her sick. She tried to turn her head to the side, but he was too strong for her.

"Do not question me, child. Or do you want to be kidnapped, too?" He spat.

"Get off me, you horrid thing," she shouted back at him. Once again, she struggled to pull herself out of his grip. Her neck grew sore. But she refused to give in.

From the corner of her eye, she noticed Dhow. The unicwhale grabbed Theo's satchel, tore it off his shoulder, and rummaged inside it. She pulled out a can of what looked like spray paint.

Dhow sprayed it like the wild unicwhale she was. Maddie and Theo watched in shock as the adninjas dropped like flies. Brazi loosened his grip on Maddie, and she ran. They couldn't believe what was happening. It was a miracle. Maddie had started to think they would never defeat them. Maddie caught Dhow's eye and nodded. Dhow smiled knowingly and continued to furiously spray the adninjas.

Brazi looked shocked. He backed off. Maddie turned to him, stuck out her tongue, and said, "Haha! We are winning. Soon we'll catch up with the kidnapper again, and this time, we won't lose him! See you later, Mr Brazi King."

And with that, Dhow sprayed a cloud of anti-adninja in his direction as they all dashed out of the maze.

CHAPTER 10

Dolphorses, Crocozebs, and Magical Mirrors

They found themselves in a long, thin corridor full of mirrors. Theo was admiring Maddie and Rabwarf, who were just ahead of him. After defeating the adninjas and leaving the maze, the tribe made their way back to the centre of the park. Rabwarf and the unicwhales said they needed to have a look from the top of the slide in order to locate the kidnapper. From that view, they could see the whole park. The kidnapper had nowhere to hide forever.

Maddie and Theo climbed to the top of the slide. They could see every corner of the park.

"I can't see him anywhere. Can you?" Maddie asked.

She knew that with his superpower the kidnapper could be hiding anywhere. They were lucky to have caught up with him earlier. If only they hadn't hesitated, things might have turned out very differently.

"Nope, I can't. Come on. Let's go see what Mr J says." Theo grabbed hold of her arm, and they jumped into a rubber ring. Theo couldn't help but feel excited about getting another go down the awesome slide. His experience was just as fabulous as it had been earlier on.

They reported back to Mr J. He decided to give Head Office a call to see if they could shed any light on the whereabouts of the kidnapper. Head Office informed him that the man had left Rainbow Slide Park and travelled to the magical mirrors.

According to Head Office, the superpower was wearing off. As the kakarooni got weaker, so did the power he gave to the kidnapper. This was excellent news for the tribe.

"I don't know why he would go to the magical mirrors. He can go further afield if he is using the secret passages," Mincha explained.

"Yes, it is only just outside Rainbow Slide Park. It doesn't make much sense unless he doesn't know how to use the passages," Dhow said.

"Well, Head Office saw him there, so let's go," Mr J said.

The kidnapper had nowhere else to go to now. If he hadn't managed to escape through Rainbow Slide Park, then all he could do was keep running.

• • •

"This place is so cool," Maddie said to Mr Rabwarf. *He's such a tiny little dwarf rabbit,* Theo thought. Rabwarf rubbed his chubby little fingers over his chin, deep in thought.

"Yes, it sure is. I have not been here before, that's for sure," he replied.

This magical mirror place sure was mystical. Theo landed here after a whirlwind whisked him off the huge water slide. It was an amazing ride, and part of the way down each member of the group was scooped up by a whirlwind. Maddie had been the first to go, so she didn't witness it. But Theo told her how fantastical it looked. Once propelled into the air, the rubber ring morphed into a small jet engine, which hurtled through the wind and the night sky.

It was late by the time they landed at the magical mirror corridor. Each of their jets landed outside in a small grassy area for parking. Once they all arrived, they wanted to have a little mooch about and investigate.

It was a strange little place. In front of the parking spaces stood a glamorous, oblong building. There were no windows on the sides, only one double door set up on a wooden platform. Golden décor laced the edges of the doors, and each had a beautiful parrot painted on the front. In fact, the whole building was decorated in a gold like Indian gold. All around the edges (where there would have been windows on a normal building), golden patterns traced the building, and each section had a different animal painted onto it. There were eagles, dragons, snakes, parrots, peacocks, and cats. These were all done with taste in multiple colours.

Above the entrance doors, a huge sign read, "Magical Mirrors." This was painted in blues, golds, and yellows. The whole thing looked like something from a circus or fairground.

Once inside they found themselves walking along a wide corridor. Each side had large mirrors lined up one after the other in a row. Each mirror was different from the next.

"Theo, this place is amazing. Look how beautiful these mirrors are. I love this one with all the lights." Maddie pointed to the mirror that caught her attention. It sparkled and shined, creating its own light.

Theo felt a little overwhelmed, but he kind of liked the place. Most of the mirrors were different in colour, shape, and size.

"I wonder why it is called 'Magical Mirrors,'" Maddie said. "They don't really look magical—a bit different, that's all." She pointed to her favourite, a pink mirror full of sparkles. It was long and thin in shape.

When she stood in front of it, Theo thought she looked a bit different. She looked like herself, but her cheeks sparkled, and stripes of vibrant colour ran through her hair like a unicorn. *Perhaps they are magical after all,* he thought.

"Which one is your favourite?" she asked Theo.

"My favourites are these three," he said, pointing to three mirrors lined up together. The middle mirror was taller, and the two on either side were the same size as one another. Each was pointed at the top. On a closer look, the middle mirror contained a large red ball of fire. It almost looked as if it were going to come alive and break out from the mirror. It looked so real.

"Theo, don't get too close," Maddie cried as she pulled him back. "You might get burnt."

The two side mirrors were black. They had cracks in the glass. Between the cracks were faint, smoky-looking skull heads. They looked a little scary to Theo. An enormous green dragon flew about in each mirror. Both dragons were identical and faced the middle mirror. With a closer look, Theo realised both dragons were breathing fire into the middle mirror.

"Come on, you pair. We need to move through here a bit quicker. You need some sleep so we can catch up with the kidnapper again bright and early." And with that Mr J sent them off to bed.

Meanwhile, Rabwarf discovered at least one of the mirrors held magical supplies. He reached his paw through the glass and retrieved a couple of sleeping bags and pillows. Maddie and Theo were both a little too excited, and neither was keen on going to sleep straight away. But they managed to have a little nose about the place, which was a bonus.

• • •

When Theo woke the next morning, he forgot where he was. It was strange sleeping in a corridor full of mirrors. Mr J and Rabwarf were asleep next to Maddie and him, but the unicwhales had left. They needed to go back to their homes for a while to refresh themselves and get a proper sleep, but had promised the tribe they would catch them up soon enough.

That morning, Theo and Maddie both felt refreshed. They had fallen straight to sleep in the end. It had been a full day yet again.

Mr J's plan was to zoom over to Head Office first thing, while the children got themselves ready. Rabwarf was certain he could get the children a fresh set of clothes from the supply mirror. He reached inside and pulled out a blue suitcase. Maddie and Theo both gasped as they recognised it straight away.

"Oh, Theo, it's the suitcase from the station." Maddie's mouth dropped open wide enough to catch a whole family of flies.

"This is too weird," he responded, shaking his head.

"Do you think that's why it was in the old carriage?" she asked as they changed into their fresh clothes.

"I guess so," he replied.

They were all set to go. Before Mr J set off, though, Maddie begged him to have a little stroll through the mirrored corridor with them.

"Please, Mr J. Just a few minutes." She fluttered her eyes. She knew this worked only too well.

He shook his head and rolled his eyes, but after some resistance, he agreed. "A quick stroll since it is on the way out, after all."

After a short walk further down the corridor, they came upon a door at the other end. It led them outside and around to the back of the building. It was a grassy area much like the front. Maddie pointed to a strange mirror planted in the middle of the grass.

"What's that?" she asked, moving towards it. Theo and Mr J joined her. Rabwarf stood back.

It was oval in shape, almost like a ball was buried into the ground with only the top being visible. It was huge. Looking up, Theo noticed quite a few more of these dotted about in the grass.

"There are loads of them," Theo announced, looking around. They were all different sizes, but this large one seemed to intrigue Maddie the most.

"There's water," she said. Theo knelt down beside her and stared into the mirror. It looked like a lake.

"Look, Maddie. It's the crocozebs and dolphorses from the kakarooni ride." He pointed to the creatures. It looked as though they were miles and miles away. The mirror made them seem distant, like there was so much depth to what they could see. And right at the bottom was the water far below everything else. As they watched, the water began to rise.

"Duck!" Theo cried. They jumped back, and within a few seconds, the lake burst out of the mirror, smashing it into tiny pieces. Water flowed everywhere, covering the grass. All the little mirrors burst too. Crocozebs and dolphorses were all around them, flapping about in the water.

The children, Mr J, and Mr Rabwarf swam frantically as the lake rushed out from the mirror.

A crocozeb hauled Maddie out of the water and dropped her into a boat. Using his mouth, he gripped her cardigan and pulled her up in one swoop. One of the dolphorses helped Theo out. She used her fin and flipped him over onto his back. Then she held him under her fin and guided his floating body to the boat. Meanwhile, Mr J and Rabwarf flapped along in the water. Once they reached the boat, Maddie held out her hand to help them climb in.

"Here, Mr J, let me help you. Grab my hand." She pulled him into the boat and then grabbed Rabwarf with a little help from the crocozeb.

It all happened so fast. Maddie and Theo both shivered from the cold water. The crocozeb who rescued Maddie had some thermal blankets, which he threw to each of the children. He was driving the boat—well, rowing, technically—so he couldn't have been much more help.

Mr J recognized the crocozeb and the dolphorse. "Croc, Delphine. How are you both? What's happening? Where are we heading?"

He and Rabwarf were used to a bit of water. They sat back and enjoyed the ride as they dried off.

"Well, Mr J, there is no need for you to go to Head Office," Croc said. "The kidnapper is not here in this magical mirror land. He is at the sea pond. That is where we have just come from. We can't go back through the mirrors, though."

"What? I was told he was here," Mr J said. He bounced over to Croc and perched himself next to the crocozeb.

"Well, you were told wrong, my friend. We need to take a trek around the zoo in the boat. It could be a long journey. Lucky for us it's a beautiful place," Croc replied. Mr J took it all in, but the children looked shocked. The plan had taken a twist yet again.

CHAPTER 11

The Mysteries of the Sea Pond

They rowed along leisurely in the small boat for a long while. It was peaceful to listen to the water and relax. Maddie and Theo chatted in the back. They were perched on the edge of a small wooden seat, which barely fit them both. It was cosy, and Maddie felt super relaxed. Her legs were crossed, and she clasped her hands behind her head. Theo, however, planted his feet firmly on the ground, poised and rigid as if waiting for something to happen. Maddie could feel the tension oozing from him.

"This is so nice, isn't it? I keep wondering what will happen next. Do you, Theo?" she asked.

"Yes, I am enjoying it too. I do keep thinking and worrying about my mum though." He turned to face her. "Do you think we will ever go home again? I really want to help catch the kidnapper, but I want to go home sometime soon as well. Don't you?"

"Don't worry so much. It will all be okay. I think we will be home again soon enough. And then you will be wishing we were back here in Imagination World." Maddie wondered why he always worried about things. He sure was her opposite, she thought.

"I know. I wish I didn't worry so much. I would like to be more like you." He blushed.

She squeezed his arm and planted a small kiss on his cheek.

Meanwhile, Mr J and Rabwarf listened to Croc and Delphine at the front of the boat. "We will be rowing all along this secret passageway. It will get us to the sea pond in the end," Croc explained.

"Yeah, we hope it won't take much longer than a few hours," Delphine added, "although it isn't as fast as the other secret passages."

Mr J would have loved to stay at the mirrors a little longer. He enjoyed it there. He told Maddie that morning how he hadn't been to that part of the zoo before and hoped it stayed and never changed. He said he wished he could take the children back there one day. He was sure they would love to investigate it further.

Maddie stood up and stretched. The boat rocked as she moved forward a little and listened to Mr J talking with Croc.

"So, is there any further news on the kidnapper? Have you spoken to Head Office?" Mr J asked.

"Nope, I don't know anything further at the moment." Croc pointed to a bend in the stretch of water. "Around the next corner is a little refreshment place. I was thinking I can moor us up there for a quick toilet break. I will call Head Office, too."

"Yes, that sounds perfect, Croc. Thank you. I'm only concerned about the kidnapper getting away again. However, I don't see where he can go now. He is trapped inside the zoo." Mr J sighed, and confusion spread across his tiny owl face. "Aw well, let's see what Head Office has to report, then."

Maddie enjoyed the boat ride. As they rowed, they saw beautiful scenery and passed under low bridges. They even saw some other boaters too. It was a very nice river for a secret passageway. The water was calm and clear.

They pulled up, and Croc moored the boat while Delphine helped them all off. Theo stretched his tense body, and Maddie took in their surroundings. She loved being on the water. But they both needed the toilet and as per usual felt ready for a bite to eat. They hadn't had any breakfast, and it was almost lunchtime. That morning had rushed past in the blink of an eye.

Maddie was in front of Theo, climbing the steps up to the restaurant. The chalkboard outside claimed they sold cheesy chips and hot chocolate. Maddie was delighted. She smiled and pointed it out to Theo.

"Yes, Theo, hot chocolate!" she told him excitedly. "And we both love cheesy chips." Theo grinned back at her.

"Mr J, can we have something to eat? We didn't have breakfast. Is there time?"

Mr J agreed. "Yes, but we can't be long."

Mr Rabwarf and Croc found a table overlooking the water while Delphine went inside with the children to use the facilities and order a few rounds of cheesy chips and hot chocolate.

It was cosy inside, a nice atmosphere with all the delights one could expect inside an English restaurant. The staff were pleasant, and the bar was well-stocked. A few other customers were seated inside the restaurant, enjoying their food and drinks.

Croc rang Head Office while they waited for their refreshments. He was relaying the latest news to Mr J and Rabwarf as Theo and Maddie returned. They took a seat and listened.

"Okay, Head Office tells me the kidnapper tried to escape. No surprise there, I guess. He foolishly decided to try and make a run for it. It was only about half an hour ago."

Theo gasped and shook his head.

"This is good news for us because now he will be paralysed for a while. Head Office put together a spell, and it must have worked. His legs won't work, and he will be stuck in one place. This gives us a chance to catch up with him."

• • •

They all felt refreshed as they headed back to the rowing boat. Maddie felt much more human after eating. She was used to eating regular meals, but it was different here in Imagination World, grabbing food as they could.

Croc assured them they weren't too far away now. Their route had them sailing past the kakarooni ride, then around to the sea pond. The route followed the pathways but couldn't be seen by anyone in the zoo except the kakaroonis. It was magic and secret, after all.

Maddie sat bolt upright as they sailed past. She couldn't believe what she saw.

"Oh, look, guys! Paul is back on his ride. He must have fixed it." She pointed across to the ride, her eyes wide with surprise.

"I thought he disappeared. He got sucked into the adninjas the last time we saw him," Theo said.

He looked happy and settled back into his job. Maddie knew he was so passionate about it. This was good news for them, knowing the ride was fixed. Hopefully, they were getting somewhere, and the king and his adninjas were losing!

"Can we stop and see if he is okay?" Maddie asked.

"No, Maddie. There is nowhere to pull in," Croc replied. "We must keep going until we hit the sea pond now. I'm sure we will find out soon enough. Paul isn't our priority right now."

Maddie was disappointed. However, she soon settled back down to relax and enjoy the rest of the ride. She and Theo sat at the back again, chatting.

"Maddie, do you think you can teach me and help me to worry less? You are so confident and full of fun. I wish I could be more like you," Theo said in a brave manner. Maddie noticed Theo seemed calmer now than the day they first met. He didn't flush every time he spoke. She had no idea how to teach or help him, but she knew how to be kind.

"Of course, I will help you as best I can. Though, I think you are great the way you are. Maybe if you can think like that, too, it will help. I simply love to have fun. Worrying is for adults, and even then, I think they worry too much." She paused for a moment. It was hard to explain what she felt inside.

"Imagine if everyone in the world stopped worrying about everything all the time. There would be so much more time to have fun and go on adventures. Don't you agree?" She tried her best to explain. She leant over and gave him a big hug. He was such a sensitive little lad. She adored this about him, and she was sure he was getting a little tougher. She enjoyed getting to know him and seeing him change.

"Thanks, Maddie. I am glad we met each other. You are okay for a girl," he said with a coy smile. *Taking his chances on being a little cheeky*, she thought.

Theo fell asleep on the last stretch of the boat ride. Maddie sat and watched him for a while. He looked peaceful. Although most of the time she was full of beans and on the go, she did appreciate some quiet chill time. She felt a lot more comfortable relaxing after the events over the last few days. Their mission had been nonstop.

There had to be a more relaxed approach to the whole thing than she was used to.

After about twenty minutes, Maddie rocked Theo on the shoulder to wake him up. It was another sunny day, and they moored up to a beautiful area. The water was crystal clear with splashes of blues and whites reflected from the sky. The only sound was the boat lapping in gentle movements against the water's edge. On approach, it seemed they had reached a good-sized pond area, which led into the sea. Around the edge of the pond, the banks were rife with green grass growing at the speed of light by the looks of it.

"The grass is tickling my knees." Maddie giggled as she stepped out of the boat. Theo held her hand as she stepped into the extremely tall grass.

The whole pond was boxed in by trees, some overlooking the water and others holding themselves back at a safe distance. Further ahead, Maddie could see an opening in the forest which led to the worldwide sea. It wasn't very wide, but she could tell it opened up. It was like the pond had an entrance, and that opening she could see ahead was the exit.

Once they all clambered out of the boat and stood on the water's edge, Maddie asked, "What's the plan? It looks deserted here."

Croc replied, "The plan, young Maddie, is to search for the kidnapper. I'm sure that much is obvious to you. I am told there are clues we will need to come across to find him. Come on, let's go this way." With that, the crocozeb led them all forward across the vast wasteland.

Maddie lagged behind a little as she was last out of the boat. She watched them all wander off. It looked odd to her. There was nothing here. She couldn't understand how the kidnapper could be here. *Where?* she thought. She stood in place for a moment, staring at the empty space. Perhaps Croc knew more than he was letting on. Or perhaps there was more than met the eye here. That wasn't unusual.

Just as she was about to follow them, she noticed a strange creature at the edge of the water. He looked like he was trying to hide or camouflage himself. She bent down to get a better look at him.

"Hello, you cute little thing. What is your name? And what even are you?" she whispered, keeping her voice low so she wouldn't reveal him. She didn't want everyone else to notice him if he was trying to hide. She was trying to spare his feelings. After meeting and getting to know Theo, she was beginning to realise not everyone was as outgoing and confident as she was. Some people liked to be cautious.

The creature tried to scamper away. He was crouched in the long grass, pulling all his limbs inwards.

"Don't be scared, mister. I won't hurt you. We are here looking for a kidnapper."

With that tiny bit of reassurance, she felt his tension loosen. Her little hand stroked his hard shell, and she felt it relax beneath her touch. He popped his head out, and his eyes flicked from side to side as he spoke. "I am a frotle," he replied. "My name is Frertle. Please be gentle with me. I am old." His little voice croaked like a frog.

He had frog eyes, arms, and legs, but his shell resembled a turtle. *He's a beautiful creature,* Maddie thought.

"Mr Frertle, I will be gentle, of course. Where do you live? Maybe I can help you get home." Maddie suggested.

"Well, that would be nice. But if you are looking for a kidnapper, I don't want to hold you up."

Theo and the others had wandered off towards the sea outlet. They hadn't noticed her absence yet.

"I need my friends to help, though. They will be kind and gentle, too. I promise." And with that, she shouted to the others to come back and help Mr Frertle. They weren't too far ahead.

"Maddie, we can't mess around," Mr J shouted back. "We need to head this way and search for the kidnapper, especially while he is paralysed. We have an advantage." But as he spoke, Maddie saw Theo running back to her.

Mr Frertle explained that he lived a mere fraction beyond the grass in his cave pond. This baffled Maddie as it looked to her like nothing but trees, grass, and water lay ahead of them.

"It's okay, Mr J. It's only over here. It is on route," she shouted back to him.

He rolled his eyes and said, "You must be quick, then."

Maddie and Theo took it in turns to carry Mr Frertle. She could tell Theo liked him, too. He was very gentle with him. They had never even seen or heard of a frotle before. It sure was an eye-opener in Imagination World, meeting all sorts of new creatures. The adventures here were so much fun.

They didn't have to walk far before Mr Frertle announced, "My home is just over there on the left." Both Maddie and Theo looked puzzled. Nothing ahead looked any different from the grass they had walked through. Maddie couldn't see anywhere for a frotle to live and especially no sign of a cave pond. Not that she really knew what a cave pond looked like.

"You may want to come into my home. I am sure my wife can help you with the kidnapper. The water whispers to her."

"What do you mean?" Maddie asked, eyes wide with astonishment.

Croc, Mr J, Mr Rabwarf, and Delphine were still ahead of them. Theo called out to them to return for a minute.

"Mr J, this is Mr Frertle's home. He says his wife can help us with the kidnapper. Can we go in and see her?" he asked.

"Mr Frertle, can you please call for your wife to come out here and share what she knows?" Mr J answered. He sounded a little annoyed. "We don't have time to mess around. But it would be very useful if she can help us."

Theo lowered Mr Frertle to the ground. The frog-like creature motioned for them to follow him. They trod through some more long grass and veered to the left. It still looked the same to Maddie.

"Very well. Stay there a moment, and I will fetch her."

Within a moment he came back.

"I'm afraid she says the waters won't tell her because it isn't for her to hear. The only way for you to hear the information is to come into the cave and hear it for yourselves." He pointed at Maddie and Theo. "She said you, Maddie and Theo, are the ones who the water will speak to."

Maddie looked at Mr J with pleading eyes and a cheeky smirk. He gave them a nod of approval to go with the frotle.

Mr Frertle waved his front arms about, trying to get them to lower onto the ground. "You need to lie on the ground like me. You won't get in the cave otherwise."

For a moment Maddie didn't know what was happening. But she soon understood what he meant and informed Theo to follow her lead. They were like slithering snakes with their stomachs flat to the ground, manoeuvring themselves forward through back-and-forth motions. Mr Frertle parted the grass with his front hands and revealed a beautiful cave pond edged with large rocks and stones. These were covered in ivy and moss. Water trickled from the top rock, dropping as a waterfall into the small pond below. The rocks acted as a roof, and as Maddie looked into the cave, it appeared to go back into a good-sized pond underneath the rocks.

Theo took one look and said, "There is no way I am going in there. I don't believe for one minute I can get into such a small space, and I am not dressed to get soaking wet." He crossed his arms and pursed his lips.

Maddie, on the other hand, was excited by the idea of a challenge. She also knew there was a possibility she could make it with magic on her side. After all, they had managed to shoot through a small watering can back in the flower gardens.

"Come on, Theo. Take my hand. It will be fine. You know you can trust me." He didn't respond, but his eyes met hers, and he sighed and took her hand. She felt his whole body shaking. She squeezed his hand for reassurance.

It was easy to enter the cave pond. Mr Frertle told them to close their eyes, stretch their arms out in front of them, and click their fingers twice. After the second click, Maddie felt her whole body shrink in an instant. When she opened her eyes, she was tiny, clad in a swimsuit, and lying in what felt like a massive lake.

It was enormous inside the cave pond. From the outside, it looked tiny. Maddie wasn't sure if magic made it bigger or if it simply was bigger than it looked. And, of course, they had shrunk.

The water felt so refreshing. Rocks made into seats and benches were scattered around the edges. Blue lights were set into the rock overhead. They illuminated the whole of the pond.

As they all emerged from the cave pond, Mr. Frertle said, "My dears, please meet my wife, Mrs Frertle, and my young frotle, Fig." Young Fig was ever so cute and looked exactly like his old father. Maddie thought Mr Frertle himself was cute, but Fig was even cuter and tinier. She wanted to keep him forever. She picked up little Fig and squeezed him so tight he almost popped. His little cheeks went red from the pressure.

"You are so cute! I want to eat you all up." She squealed with delight. "Oh, sorry. I didn't mean to hurt you," she said, popping him back down.

"Don't worry. He is tough as old boots, Maddie." Mr Frertle giggled.

They sat on the rock seats overlooking the pond. Maddie thought it was so beautiful in there. The water glistened under the blue lighting, and the trickling of the fountain outside on the rocks was soft and peaceful like background music.

"Okay, children, you need to jump into the water and listen," Mrs Frertle said. "The water whispers, and so far it has always been correct. Go over to the corner where the entrance of the cave is. Put your ears to the water and wait."

Maddie and Theo didn't wait to be told twice. They jumped in and followed her instructions. It wasn't long until they heard something. It was a soft whisper.

"Maddie, Theo, the kidnapper is about to head back to Rainbow Slide Park. Brazi has told him he can escape from there. He is leaving the sea pond very soon, so you must be fast. He may be paralysed, but Brazi is helping him move."

· · ·

Maddie and Theo thanked the Frertles and left the sea pond cave quick smart. Once they got outside, their old clothes replaced the swimsuits.

Maddie pointed into the distance. "Oh, look over there. What are those large stones? I don't remember seeing them before."

"Never mind those for a minute. What did the water whisper to you?" Mr J asked her. Maddie repeated what she heard.

"Then I need to take a trip to Head Office. I didn't get there when we left the magical mirrors. I have this feeling something isn't quite right." He shuddered as he looked Maddie directly in the eyes.

"Wait, Mr J. I heard something else, too. The water whispered to me. It said Paul might need some help."

They all stared at Theo, unsure what to make of this. Theo assured them nothing else was said.

As Mr J left for Head Office, the others walked over toward the large stones.

"I think we should go and investigate those stones, for sure," Rabwarf said.

"Yes, he could be trying to hide somewhere he thinks is safe," Delphine added.

As they neared the large stone area, Maddie gasped. "Wow, they look amazing. Look how they are all in a circle."

There were large stones the size of trees, and in between each of the larger stones, a smaller one was nestled. It was like a family—a child stone accompanied by an adult. All in all, there were twelve stones. Maddie wondered if there was a purpose for them. They seemed to be randomly placed here in the middle of nowhere. The rest of the sea pond area was deserted. Aside from water and grass, nothing else seemed to be here. Only empty space.

Maddie's face dropped. As they had reached the stones, it became obvious no one else was here. Were they always going to be one step behind? It sure felt like it.

"Maddie, I've had enough of this now," Theo murmured. "I don't think we are ever going to catch up with the kidnapper. He is too quick for us. I want to go home. I can't take any more."

Maddie was a little concerned by Theo crashing like this. He looked as though he was about to burst into tears. She felt sorry for him.

"It's okay, Theo. I think we are really close to catching him. Let's not give up now we have gotten this far." She pulled him into a tight hug. She knew simply loving someone was one of the best ways to help them. "Come on. You have been a great help to me. I think we make a good team, don't you? We have Mr J and Rabwarf and all the wonderful people we have met along the way helping us, too. I think things can only get better from now on."

"I'm sorry, Maddie. I've just had enough, and it's all getting too much. I'm sure I will be okay. I know you are right. Thank you." He smiled and seemed a little better. Maddie wasn't going to let him give up.

• • •

Mr J returned from Head Office. He looked stressed. His feathers were all ruffled, and he spoke fast, barely stopping for breath.

"Guys, I have bad news. The green men are tied up at Head Office. We need to help."

Maddie's eyes widened. "Oh no, what are we going to do, Mr J? We need to go and rescue them." She noticed Theo close his eyes and bow his head.

Maddie grasped his shoulder and gave him a reassuring look, one that said, *it will be fine. We will get through this as well.*

"I am going to need you all to come to Head Office with me. Yes, we need to rescue them. They have been tied up ever since the kakarooni ride crashed. They are fine though. They are locked in a room, and I could only talk to them through the window. It's—"

"But Mr J, what about Brazi?" Theo interrupted. "Won't he be there, trying to catch us?"

"He was nowhere to be seen, and neither were the other workers," Mr J explained. "I couldn't get into the room on my own. But we need to act fast before Brazi returns."

"But what are we going to do about the kidnapper, Mr J?" Maddie asked. Of course, she wanted to go and help rescue the green men, but she also feared the kidnapper would escape before they got to him.

"Don't worry. I have a plan. We are going to pick up Paul on the way. I have this feeling he could help us, and maybe we can find out what help he needs." Mr J hurried them along as he spoke.

"That's a great idea. Paul will be such a good help," Rabwarf said.

"It all makes sense now, why Head Office has been giving us strange information," Mr J said, rambling on. "Brazi made them say what he wanted us to hear. If we can get the green men untied, there will be a way we can at least delay the kidnapper. In fact, we are much better off going to Head Office than we are chasing the kidnapper right now. We need Head Office back on board."

Maddie agreed. "Let's go."

Croc and Delphine decided to stay at the sea pond and wait there for them. They thought it best in case they heard anything through the waters.

Mr J's wings expanded as they did when he carried them on his back. His whole body grew five times its original size, and seats appeared on each of his wings for them all to sit on. Maddie, Theo, and Rabwarf clambered on and got themselves comfy.

• • •

It was early afternoon when they reached the kakarooni ride. Maddie saw Paul glance towards them from his window. Everyone was strapped in and ready to go, and he was about to begin his next ride. Mr J waddled over to the kakarooni ride. Paul jumped out of his seat and stepped out of the ride to see what was happening.

"Mr J, what brings you here?" he asked as he approached the little owl. The children and the others stood back. They were happy to let Mr J handle this one although Maddie could hear all the conversation from where they were.

"Paul, how are you, old fella? I need your help." Mr J reached out, and Paul shook his little wing, smiling.

"The green men are tied up at Head Office," Mr J explained. "I have the rest of the guys with me, and we are going to rescue them. Please, will you come too? The more help we have, the better. As soon as we can rescue them, the sooner we can stop the kidnapper escaping." He crossed his little bird wings and looked up at Paul with pleading eyes.

Paul stared straight ahead. His mouth dropped open, and his eyes grew wide.

"Mr J, I can't just..."

"I know I'm asking a lot. You have innocently gotten mixed up in all this, but I know you have a big heart. Paul, I am desperate." He moved his little wings in front of him, clasping them together, and cocked his head to one side.

"Mr J, I really want to help, and I wish I could. But I don't feel I can get involved. I've already had enough trouble with that horrible King Brazi." He sighed. "Please, can you manage without me? I have these people to take on the ride, too. Your timing couldn't have been worse."

"I understand," Mr J said, lowering his head. He sloped off to the tribe as Paul hopped back into his ride. Maddie couldn't believe he was walking away from them. She ran over to the ride and tapped on the window before Paul had a chance to take off.

"Please, Paul, we need you." She begged through the window, her eyes about to spill over in a flood of tears.

He sighed but jumped back out of the cabin. He took her hands in his and softly explained, "Maddie, I'm sorry I can't help. As I explained to Mr J, it hasn't been long since my ride got fixed, and I want to keep my head down and do my job. Brazi is not a nice adninja to cross, and I have to live here."

"But if you help us, you will be rid of Brazi altogether, which will make your life easier," Maddie explained. She watched him think about it.

"Maddie, please don't ask this of me," he begged.

"But you know it makes sense. It will help everything be better." She hugged him tight.

He shook his head. "I can't help. I'm sorry." He ripped her arms from around his waist and made his way back to his ride.

She stared after Paul, those earlier tears escaping her eyes. She looked down at her feet as she tucked her arms around herself and moved back to the others, shuffling herself along the freshly cut grass. She was almost back with the others when she heard Paul shout, "Maddie, wait!" She turned round to see him running towards her. She ran to him and grabbed his hand. They joined the others.

"I told my passengers what happened. They said I needed to help." His grin was wide.

Maddie was so happy and grateful that Paul changed his mind. They would struggle without his help.

"Oh, one minute. I almost forgot something." He ran back to the ride. He had a girl's purse in his hand.

"What is that for?" she asked.

He tapped his nose and said, "Never you mind."

They all clambered back onto Mr J once he expanded. It wasn't a long journey to Head Office.

It was such a peaceful, still afternoon. The sky was bright blue with the odd cloud, and the birds chirped away. It made for a glorious ride. There was a slight breeze in the air, too, but Maddie found it quite refreshing as it rushed past her face. Mr J flew at great speed. He was in a hurry to get back to the green men.

On the way, Paul told them how he managed to escape Brazi's clutches and fix his ride with the help of the kakaroonis.

"The everchanging buildings move, as you know. I figured if I was brave enough and jumped at the right time, I would make it out. I watched the pattern of how they changed and realised the door to where I was locked in had a small gap, and I had a few seconds to jump through."

"Weren't you scared of falling through the gap?" Maddie asked.

"Absolutely I was, but I knew I at least had to give it a shot. It was a better option to fall through the gap than stay locked up forever."

"Oh, wow. You are so brave, Paul," Theo said. He looked very impressed. "I'm so glad you escaped."

"Paul, what do you need help with? The waters whispered to Theo. Let us help you," Maddie said, taking his hand in hers. His eyes welled up.

"Maddie, you wouldn't understand, but thank you for being kind," he answered.

"I might. I am a wise eight-year-old, you know," she replied with her air of Maddie confidence. Paul laughed.

"Well, it's my daughter," he explained. "I miss her so much. I wish there were a way I could see her, but she lives in the real world."

Maddie's heart felt heavy as lead. She wasn't sure how to help, and there was no time to respond as they landed at Head Office.

It had all changed since the last time the children were there. Maddie noticed all the buildings were different and remembered how often they changed the last time, too. This time she didn't see any of the little wizard men. In fact, the streets were quiet and deserted. Maddie wondered where they all were.

Mr J voiced his plan. "I think you guys should stay here and keep a lookout for Brazi or anyone suspicious. Paul and I will go and see about rescuing the green men. Then, if we need your help, we can come back for you." The others nodded in agreement and watched Paul and Mr J stride away.

• • •

Maddie, Theo, and Rabwarf didn't wait long for Mr J and Paul to return. No surprise adninjas or Brazi had turned up. Rabwarf kept a close eye everywhere. The children tried their best, but they were so mesmerised with the everchanging buildings that it was difficult to concentrate at times.

When they returned, Mr J explained what had happened at Head Office.

"The green men had nodded off. We had to knock on the window to get their attention."

"They told Mr J he would need to smash the door or window in," Paul said. "It was locked. But I had another idea. Earlier on, one of the children on my ride dropped her purse. A couple of hair grips were inside it. I once saw someone on a film unpick a lock with those, and I always wondered if it would work."

Oh, so that's why he grabbed the purse, Maddie thought.

"It took a few tries, and the grips are not going to be of much use now to anyone's hair. But we got inside. The lock turned, releasing the handle. So, in we went. Admittedly, I looked back to check no one was coming. I was convinced that King Brazi might appear at any moment." His eyes were fixed on the children.

"The untying of the green men was the easy bit," Mr J said, continuing to relay the story. "I don't know how we are going to keep Brazi and his adninjas away. The green men plan to create a spell to prevent the kidnapper from leaving Rainbow Slide Park, but keeping Brazi away will be difficult. There's no way they could create spells with him lingering about."

"And we need to find a way to protect the green men," Paul added.

Rabwarf had been telling the children about an idea he had. He raised his paw to speak, but Maddie screamed before he could.

"There is trouble, Mr J. Look over there. I see a wispy shadow person. He is heading right for the green men's office! It's Brazi! What are we going to do?"

CHAPTER 12

The Enchanted Forest

"Brazi!" Mr J shouted as he ran over to the adninja king. "What are you up to? Don't even bother going in there. The green men are free. You are too late!" Brazi wasn't alone. At least ten adninjas floated around him. They sure did freak Maddie out, all floaty and wispy with their spooky eyes.

As Mr J approached Brazi, Maddie tapped Rabwarf on his shoulder and whispered, "I think you need to make the plan go ahead." Rabwarf nodded and disappeared while Brazi and Mr J continued arguing.

"Well, in that case, I shall have to tie and lock them up again. You silly Jamaican owl fool. It won't be a difficult task. I keep telling you. I will always win." Brazi's voice dripped with anger.

"You are never going to defeat me and the kidnapper. You couldn't even manage to find him at the sea pond when he was right under your nose. Too busy playing with the frotles. Bunch of idiots you are!" He spat.

Before Mr J could answer, Maddie saw Rabwarf return. He wasn't gone long, but he explained to the children it would only take the flick of a switch in the other main room.

"Mr Brazi," Rabwarf shouted, "I think you will find that in about one minute's time, everything you see before you will disappear. Goodbye!"

Rabwarf ran towards Mr J and grabbed him. "We need to leave. There is no time to explain."

And with that, they all clambered onto Mr J's expanded body. He flew off the ground as Head Office began to disappear before their eyes. He hovered for a few minutes so the children could watch. It was fascinating. Maddie and Theo were mesmerised.

Sparks flew into the air like giant fireworks. The stupid adninjas and Brazi were flung into the air. A big flash of lightning streaked across the sky, and the world around them darkened. None of them could see anything. But they felt themselves being tossed about. Mr J frantically flapped his wings to get them moving.

Brazi and the adninjas managed to keep themselves afloat. They laughed their wispy heads off at Mr J. He wasn't prepared for this. The explosion caught him off guard, which was a blessing for Brazi. He took complete advantage of the situation.

Theo watched as Brazi produced a wand and pointed it towards them. The last thing he heard was the king shouting, "Alakazaroo!"

• • •

Maddie woke feeling a little dazed. Her neck was sore from sleeping all twisted up. She tried to come around and remember what happened. Why were they lying in a heap on the ground? Theo was next to her in his seat. They were all still strapped onto Mr J, but he was collapsed on the ground. She looked over at Paul and Rabwarf. They were both unconscious, too. Mr J looked totally mashed. He was sprawled out, and his body was squashed flat to the ground like a fly that had been stepped on by a human.

She stretched her hands above her head and rocked from side to side a few times to ease the tension in her neck a little. She decided to leave them all for a bit to come around when they were ready. She hoped everyone was okay and checked they were all still breathing before she left. It was a big fall from the sky as Head Office disappeared underneath them. All she remembered was twirling down and down. Then it felt like something was sprinkled under her nose. She remembered breathing it in and passing out. Well, that's what she assumed because the next thing she knew, she was waking up.

They were in some kind of forest. Evening was approaching, and the sky had gotten a little dusky. The surroundings were beautiful. Maddie loved the forest. It was a magical place, and this one was very different from the average forest.

All of a sudden the whole place was overcome with light. Before Maddie's eyes, the forest lit up into a thousand beautiful, spectacular colours.

"Wowee," she whispered.

Two nearby trees served as posts, and stretched high up across their branches, a sign read, "Enchanted Electric Forest." It was written in a funky calligraphic font, and the letters were multi-coloured. Above the lettering was a picture of a golden fox with wings that stretched the width of the sign. On each tree, there was an owl, both of which lit up into bright colours. The owls' eyes glowed as if they were alive, staring directly into Maddie. And all the other trees around her sprung to life with colour. Colourful lanterns hung from some of the trees, too, giving the whole place that extra sparkle.

Off to her right, Maddie noticed a bridge hidden in the dense bushes. Pulling her shirt snug to protect herself from the evening breeze, she made her way over to it.

The pathway leading to the bridge was illuminated by lights in the shapes of lotus flowers and animals. All were scattered around the edges. It was a spectacular sight.

As Maddie got to the bridge, she realised it looked like one of those train carriages, the type often seen in a children's theme park. It resembled a toy train that rides around the park so all areas can be visited. There were no windows. Rather, it had wooden slats on the sides.

The bridge was like that, complete with a wooden open-slat roof. Like all the other lit parts of the forest, this bridge was multi-coloured. Each panel glowed a different colour. It arched itself across a small lake, providing access to the other side of the forest.

Maddie grew excited about the prospect of further exploration here in this beautiful forest. Before she crossed the bridge, she stopped in her tracks and stared across to the other side of the lake. Leaning both her arms onto the ledge, she cupped her cheeks in her hands. The view was mind-boggling. Trees outlined the lake, but because they were illuminated, their reflections on the water were extra beautiful and captivating. The colours were out of this world (literally), and they sparkled and shimmered all across the lake, making pretty patterns.

She stayed in this position for a good while, soaking in the atmosphere and the view all around her. She decided against heading over the bridge and instead turned on her heel and went back to the others.

Theo was stirring when she returned.

"What is this place? What happened, Maddie?" he asked, looking around.

Paul and Rabwarf were asleep, and so was Mr J.

"I don't know, Theo. But it is a beautiful forest. Look at the lights. Aren't they amazing? I've been off investigating a little bit." As he came round, he looked about at what Maddie was describing.

She continued, "I think we need to be in Rainbow Slide Park though. I'm worried the kidnapper is going to escape. I wish the others would wake up. Do you think we should wake them?" As usual, Maddie spoke a mile a minute in all her excitement, thinking about everything all at once.

"Slow down, Maddie. Let's think this through a little, shall we?" Theo replied.

"I know you are right, Theo. It's just such a lovely place, and I want to wander over the bridge and explore. But I think we need to catch the kidnapper first. I hope one day we can come back to this imagination world and explore the whole lot."

"Yes, we need to catch him once and for all now. Remember, Rabwarf said the green men are going to create another spell to stop the kidnapper if he does try to escape Rainbow Slide Park. I think we should wake the others and get on."

Maddie nodded her head and moved towards Paul and Rabwarf. They were sprawled flat on the ground.

"Do you think one day we will get to come back here?" Theo asked, letting himself go a little. "It would be amazing." Maddie felt such a difference in him since the beginning of this quest. He was a lot more comfortable around her. She was proud of him for being braver. Some of the things they had to face had helped him a lot, too, she realised. Brazi and his challenges had been good for him.

"Yes, it would. I hope we can." She smiled, shaking Paul and Rabwarf a little.

"Wake up," she said. "It's Maddie."

Paul and Rabwarf woke without much struggle. However, Mr J wouldn't come round. Maddie felt concerned. Her pulse raced faster than ever before as her nerves increased. She loved Mr J so much and hoped he was going to be okay, but it seemed whatever Brazi did had hit him hard.

Rabwarf grabbed Theo's satchel and reached inside for the medicine. He knew the medicine could be used for all sorts of things. He only hoped saving Mr J was one of those uses. Rabwarf spooned some medicine into Mr J's mouth. This was a task in itself as he was sprawled on his side, his mouth proving difficult to access. Now all they had to do was wait.

• • •

They couldn't do a great deal to help while Mr J was still unconscious. Maddie felt utterly useless.

"Come on, kids. We will go and find something to eat," Paul said.

"Well, you could always gather me some firewood while you are out," Rabwarf said with a smile. "That would help. It would help Mr J to keep him as warm as possible. Don't be too long. I will try and get a fire started with the few bits around here."

"That's a great idea. We want to help." Theo smiled at Rabwarf.

They left Rabwarf to nurse Mr J and scrambled about for some wood. Maddie was super keen to show them both the amazing bridge, and she also couldn't wait to cross it and see what delights enticed them across the water. Luckily, Paul and Theo were both feeling stronger, and they loved this enchanted forest as much as Maddie. It seemed only Mr J was affected in a bad way. They hoped he would pull through, but there was not much they could do by sitting around watching him and waiting.

Across the bridge, they found even more beautiful glowing forestry. In front of them was a set of stone steps. Excitement driving her as usual, Maddie ran straight for the first step.

"I wonder where these lead to. Can we go this way?" she asked the other two.

"Yeah, let's go. I can see lanterns." Theo pointed ahead.

He was right. At the top of the steps, a huge meadow amid a cluster of trees appeared. As they reached the top, Maddie squealed in delight. A number of colourful lanterns hung above their heads. They looked up in awe. Maddie loved lights. And these were extra special. They seemed to hang from the sky.

"Wow, look at all these lights. This place is so beautiful! I don't want to leave. It's getting better and better the more areas we land in. I want to stay locked in Imagination World forever," Maddie said with all the enthusiasm in Imagination World.

"It sure is beautiful," Paul answered. "But be careful what you ask for, Maddie. Why do you think I am still here?"

Maddie frowned. "I don't know, Paul. So, are you trapped here? I thought you were in someone's dream. Oh, please do tell us."

"Come on, let's see if we can find something to eat. Then we can sit, and I'll tell you the story. Theo, come along, lad," he said as he turned back. Theo still stood in place, staring at the lanterns.

Together they made their way back down the steps. Maddie skipped up to Paul and slipped her tiny hand into his. She liked him, and she felt a little closer to him since learning about his daughter. She was eight years old, too. She felt him squeeze her hand. He looked down at her and smiled. It was nice. She felt the urge to hug him tight and make all his pain go away, but for now, she merely smiled back.

Theo walked beside her. She grabbed his hand, too. He was used to that now. They all skipped into the forest, taking Maddie's lead. She loved skipping.

They came across a tiny pixie hut. They had a great little menu—not the usual burger and chips they had been eating the last few days. Here they offered pixie twist salads, wraps, and homemade mud pie. Maddie thought it was a strange little place, and because it was so small, they had to crouch down to order their food. Theo and Maddie both opted for a wrap while Paul was more adventurous and asked to try the mud pie. He was a lot more used to some of the strange eating habits in Kakarooni Zoo.

There were tables, but they too were miniscule. The pixies said they could shrink their bodies if they wanted to sit and eat, so they went for it. It was fun being shrunk twice in one day. There weren't any other people about in the forest. However, being this size opened up a whole new world of pixies and fairies.

"Wow, now that we are small like fairies we can see them all," Theo commented, taking in their new surroundings.

"So, come on, Paul. Tell us why you are here," Maddie said as soon as they sat down.

"Well, I was living back in the real world, and I had a strange dream one night. I dreamt I was driving a train. But you know what dreams are like, all a bit mixed up." He raised his eyes.

"So, as I was driving the train, the scene shifted to a deserted railway. I crashed the train and flew from the window onto the track. When I woke up within the dream, there was a carriage to my left that had survived the wreck. I hauled myself onto the carriage to rest a bit." He sighed. Maddie and Theo stared at him, lost for words.

"Then something really strange happened inside that carriage. I can't explain it. But there were sparks and flashing lights and all sorts of weird nonsense. The next thing I remember is waking up at Head Office."

Maddie looked at Theo, and she knew they shared the same thought. It must have been the same deserted railway and carriage that they came through. Although for some reason, Paul entered through a dream.

Maddie gasped. "Paul, that's exactly how we got here. What did the carriage look like?" she asked, still reeling from the shock. Maddie couldn't believe what she was hearing.

"It was full of graffiti. The seats inside the carriage were ripped to shreds, but everything was in place. The windows were small, so it was pretty dark and dingy in there—damp as well. The smell of mildew was extremely noticeable."

"Did you see a suitcase?" Maddie asked.

"Umm, yes, there was a blue one on the front seat. I never did get to open it to see what was inside because no sooner had I hauled myself up than I was catapulted to Head Office." As he spoke, they each finished off their food.

Maddie jumped in. "The same thing happened to us. Right, Theo?" She glanced over at him, and he nodded.

"We thought we were the only ones who came to this world. What about all the other children here?" she asked.

"They are imaginary, Maddie," Paul said. "I have been here for a year now, and I am used to strange things. It isn't really a surprise to me how you got here."

"This is so cool!" Maddie beamed.

"But Paul, how did you end up staying and working here on the kakarooni ride?" Theo asked.

"When I landed at Head Office, the green men were a little shocked to see me. They didn't anticipate any humans being able to enter this world. Adults never believe in magic or make-believe, and they can't enter without this belief. At the least, they must arrive with someone who does believe. The green men couldn't even speak English then, so I struggled to communicate with them."

Theo gasped. "They didn't speak English?"

"Nope. One of the workers there could speak a little, so he helped with translation. I slept in a room at Head Office for a while. It was comfy enough for me to get my head down, and they fed me. It was a strange few months, and all I wanted was to get back to reality. But the green men begged me to stay for a while and help get this ride off the ground—the kakarooni ride."

"Why didn't you want to leave?" Theo asked. Maddie listened to his story with complete fascination.

"I didn't see much choice. I had no idea how to leave this world. So, for the next few months I helped get the ride up and running and, in return, Head Office built me a little hut to live in. I'm happy enough, apart from missing my daughter. Hopefully, one day I will be able to go back to reality and see her."

"Paul, we know how you can leave this world. Don't we, Maddie?" Theo said.

Maddie nodded her head and let Theo continue. Theo told him about the yellow flower portals.

"Yes, I know about them. I've tried it, but it has never worked for me," Paul said, shaking his head.

"Maybe there is more to them than we think. We will have to ask the unicwhales," Maddie said.

"Yes, perhaps we can. So, you see, I'm stuck here for now. But I don't mind. I've gotten used to my life here, and I enjoy it for the most part." He sighed. "Maybe there is a way we can make these imagination worlds real. Then I could see my daughter again.

"If you do ever get out, maybe you can give my daughter a message for me. Please find her and tell her I love her."

Maddie saw sadness in his eyes. She saw the lump rise in his throat as he tried to swallow it down. She wished she could take away his pain.

"Of course I will, Paul." She smiled at him, then leant in and kissed his cheek.

• • •

Mr J was awake when they returned. Maddie was so pleased. When she saw Mr J standing, she ran up to him and gave him a big squeeze.

"I love you, Mr J. I'm glad to see you awake and getting better. I was so worried about you."

He was still not too good, but the medicine was helping him heal. He had a big bruise on his head, and his leg had a nasty cut. His legs weren't very big at all, and the cut ran almost all the way down his left leg. Rabwarf had found some leaves in the forest, which he knew helped the cut to heal.

"Oooh, what a lovely warm fire, Rabwarf." Maddie rubbed her hands over the flames. Paul and Theo had managed to pick up a few more pieces of wood on their walk back, which they threw into the small blaze.

"Yes, it sure helps," Rabwarf said.

Mr J looked a bit dopey. He wasn't in a state to fly or walk about to catch the kidnapper. But he was keen to know what happened. Rabwarf explained. "Well, Mr J, while you and Paul were rescuing the green men, I remembered a top-secret division of Head Office. The unicwhales told me about it—only they know about it. I'm afraid it was I who caused all the mass destruction." Rabwarf closed his eyes for a second and hung his head low.

"The flicking of a switch, which transported the green men to that top-secret division, triggered the explosion. I am sorry. But it is good for the green men to be protected. Everything is set up the same for them at the new office." He looked Mr J in the eye as he explained.

"Ah, I see." Mr J didn't have much to say, so he nodded his head. Maddie was sure Mr J understood Rabwarf's intentions. He wasn't better yet and didn't have much energy to talk.

It was getting late, so everybody agreed it would be best to camp in the forest for the night. This would give Mr J time to heal. They had every faith the kidnapper wouldn't get very far overnight either. They knew Head Office was getting on well because Rabwarf gave them a call. The spell was almost sorted. They only needed to finalise a few details through the night. Head Office assured them the kidnapper wasn't going anywhere. They had closed all the secret passages off so it would take him forever to get to the other side of Rainbow Slide Park.

Maddie and Theo weren't ready to sleep yet. They wanted to investigate the forest further. Rabwarf, Paul, and Mr J, who were all happy to chill for a bit, stayed put while Maddie and Theo went off into the forest.

"Paul and I will set up some kind of camp to sleep overnight," Rabwarf said. "I also have a fairy friend who may help out."

The children were both excited about this. They both loved camping with a passion, even Theo with his fussy, anxious ways.

Maddie and Theo ventured back across the bridge and into the illuminated forest. It was almost eight p.m., so they promised Rabwarf they wouldn't be more than an hour so they could get a good rest for tomorrow. The plan for the following day was to get to Rainbow Slide Park and face the kidnapper and King Brazi once and for all. There would likely be a big fight or showdown of some sort, hopefully the result being a returned kakarooni.

Upon returning to the others, Maddie and Theo were pleasantly surprised to see the camp Rabwarf and Paul had set up. Rabwarf confessed his fairy friends had helped him. The fire still burned, keeping them all warm and lit. A chill nipped at the late evening air. But the fire crackled, hissed, and glowed, creating light and sound along with the warmth.

Paul and Rabwarf made a makeshift tent for the children out of some old tarpaulin scraps. They tied it up between the trees to provide them with cover. It was cosy inside, thanks to the fairies who helped Rabwarf find some bedding. Not only could the fairies shrink things with their magic dust, but they could also make things bigger. One of the fairies had some spare bedding in her little fairy house. So, she sprinkled magic dust on it and gave it to Rabwarf. Their sleep would no doubt be lovely and cosy tonight. Rabwarf and Paul even took the trouble of collecting lots of branches to provide them with a little bit of cushion.

They were all settled in for the night when Head Office contacted Mr J.

CHAPTER 13

Whirlwinds, Swings, and the Cheese Board

Theo woke to something tickling his nose. Assuming it was some forest creature, he tried to swat it away with his hand. He'd had a comfy night's sleep with Maddie tucked up next to him. He was surprised, but the branches made a softer base than he expected. It was a little chilly that night, but with Maddie clinging to him, he kept warm.

He opened his eyes and was shocked to see there was no little forest creature. It was an adninja. He leapt out of the bed screaming, waking everyone else in the camp. The adninja floated off.

"The adninjas are back! Quick, they are going to attack. I'm sure of it!"

They all took a minute to come around and realise what he was saying. Within a few seconds, everyone was wide awake. A moment later the adninja returned with a team of his floaty friends.

The wispy creatures began to cause havoc in the camp. They ripped down the tarpaulin and threw all the fire logs about. In a frenzy, they tore up the bedsheets, too. Their spooky eyes were wide with desire—a desire to destroy.

One of them spoke. "My master says I must destroy you all."

"You are never going to destroy us," Maddie shouted without an ounce of fear. "This is a dream world; we can't die. But we will destroy you! We aren't afraid of you silly adninjas."

Theo soon realised they would have another fight on their hands. The adninjas didn't look as though they intended to give up in a hurry.

They continued to upturn the campsite and attack the children in the process. But Maddie and Theo were too fast for them. They ducked and dived to avoid any confrontation. Mr J kept himself out of the way in a cluster of bushes.

The same adninja spoke again. "I have a message from my master. You must come to Rainbow Slide Park immediately. The kidnapper and kakarooni will be out of the zoo by the time you reach them, but he wants to meet with you. Be there at ten."

"We will be there." Mr J squawked from his hiding place.

"Bring the money and you will get the kakarooni back. Meet him at the cheese board."

"What is the cheese board?" Theo asked.

"I will explain to you on the way," Mr J said.

The adninjas floated away. They had only come to deliver their message, but they seemed to enjoy trashing the camp for a bit of fun.

Once they were gone, Mr J shuffled out into the clearing.

"The call from Head Office last night was to warn me the adninjas might attack. But the good news is the green men have managed to cast another spell. Brazi is about to try to break the kidnapper out, but if he tries to leave, he will be wiped off his feet again."

"Why doesn't Brazi simply leave with the kakarooni?" Maddie asked.

"Because any creatures of Kakarooni Zoo won't last outside of it for more than a few hours unless they have another dream world to enter," Rabwarf said.

While Mr J left to call Head Office, Rabwarf and the children tidied up and built a new fire so he could cook them all a little breakfast. It was still early, so they had enough time to fill their tummies before they faced Brazi and the kidnapper, hopefully for the final time.

The news from Head Office was extremely useful. Mr J relayed it.

"The kidnapper tried to escape, but the spell kicked in and knocked him off his feet," he said. "This is brilliant news. He knows he is defeated now. They can't do much else. Brazi has lost power." Mr J laughed when he told them all.

"Do you think he will still try to get money from us?" Maddie asked.

"I doubt it. Brazi will be so mad. He doesn't have the upper hand anymore. How the tables have turned." Mr J smirked.

After breakfast, Rabwarf marched them all off to his fairy friend's house. The fairy, Angus, had access to a magical swing hanging from the tree he lived in. If it reached high enough, this swing created a massive whirlwind around the branch. This whirlwind would whisk them away to wherever they wished to go. They simply had to say the magic words while Angus sprinkled his dust. He shrunk them all, and once they were tiny, the swing was big enough for them all to sit together.

Mr J chanted, "Take us to the cheese board."

• • •

As they travelled through the whirlwind, Mr J explained what the children should expect. "So, there is a giant cheese board game. It sometimes appears in Rainbow Slide Park. I don't know why Brazi wants to meet us there, but I think you will be amazed by it, so it is worth going if only for you to see it." He rubbed his chin feathers in wonderment.

They landed a few meters from the entrance of the cheese board. Both Maddie and Theo looked at the enormous board in disbelief.

"It looks like twice the size of a football pitch or maybe even bigger," Theo said. He had been to a couple of football matches with Tim. "It's massive."

Everything on the board looked double its normal size, too. After seeing tiny frotle and fairy homes, this giant's world was completely bizarre, magical, and thrilling all at the same time.

Mr J and the children jumped off the swing together, and they were greeted by Croc, Delphine, and the three unicwhales: Mincha, Artcru, and Dhow.

"What are you all doing here?" Maddie asked, intrigued. Tears of happiness shimmered in her eyes. "We've missed you. But we've also had so much fun. Haven't we, Theo?" She ran and cuddled them all at once.

"We have come to help you once and for all. We want to help fight off the horrid King Brazi and free the kakarooni," Croc replied.

"Yeah, and we love cheese too! Even giant pieces are yummy to munch on," Delphine added, causing them all to burst into laughter.

Maddie shed a little a tear. "Isn't it wonderful that they are all here to help us, Theo?"

He nodded, feeling a little choked up himself. The wonderful creatures they had met throughout Kakarooni Zoo was one of the most amazing parts of their whole experience here. Everyone had been so helpful. It was a shame the green men weren't here. But Theo had a feeling they hadn't seen the last of them.

Theo gently walked over to the large cheese board to take a closer look. He turned to see Maddie running up to him.

She cuddled into his shoulder with her usual excitement and bubbly energy while Theo eyed the cheese board with hunger. It was more of a hunger to explore it all than a desire to eat it. The board was extremely long, a lot longer in length than width, and it was split into square sections. He couldn't see it all properly, but it looked as though there were three squares across and at least five or six from the front to the back. It was similar to a chess board, alternating black and white squares.

However, rather than chess pieces, the board was covered in all the foods one might find on a cheese board. The first square of the front row had grapes, crackers were on the second, and the furthest square to their right had goats' cheese.

Theo saw many different supersized foods and some animals too. "Look at that goat," he said to Maddie, pointing to the goats' cheese square.

"Oh, I would love to feed and stroke the goats. And Theo, look at the back. Is that chocolate?" Maddie licked her lips as a huge grin spread across her face.

It was all very random, Theo thought, all the different foods thrown together on a large black-and-white-squared board.

"Isn't this cheese board simply amazing? I want to go play on it and eat all the nice bits. Do you think Brazi will be long?" she asked Theo in her super-excited-Maddie way.

"It does look interesting. Although, the goats look a bit scary."
A shiver rippled through Theo's body.

"Maybe we can ask Mr J if we can have a play on it while we
wait," she suggested.

Theo agreed they should at least ask him. They did have a few
minutes spare.

The children walked back to Mr J and all the others. He was
busy telling them about Head Office and the fall. He had pretty
much recovered now and was back to his jolly, wise owl self. Theo
was worried about Mr J. He had come to idolise him, and he feared
what might happen if he lost Mr J.

"I don't want to spoil your fun, children, but I think we should
wait for the king. We need to get this all sorted now. I've had
enough of chasing him and the kidnapper about," Mr J said. The
children were a bit disappointed, but they knew he was right.

They didn't have to wait much longer for King Brazi. He soon
floated in with his wispy sidekicks, looking as confident as ever.

"Mr J, Rabwarf, children, and all you others, whoever you are.
It's a pleasure, as always. I look forward to exchanging money and
kakaroonis with you." A ghastly smile curled his lips. "Now, show
me the cash, and we can begin."

"You have to be kidding me, Brazi. You think I'll simply hand
over money to you? What is your game? You are a fool. Hand them
over to us now and let this be an end to it all," Mr J said.

"There will be no hard feelings. But we are sick of all the
chasing about. Do the right thing for once, King Brazi." He stood
mere inches from the spooky, wispy shadow of a man. The children
were within hearing distance, but they stayed out of the way, leaving
Mr J to deal with Brazi.

"You have no chance, Mr J. If I did that, then yes, you're right. I
would be a fool. But I am no fool. You may think you are winning,
but you do not know as much as you think you do." He couldn't
continue for laughing that evil Brazi laugh.

"What do we not know?" Mr J shouted. "Come on, Brazi. Spit
it out and hurry up. We only want the kakarooni. Then we can all
get on with our day. These children need to return to their reality
world.

"The kakarooni will die soon if he doesn't get to the Cold Library. Do you really want that on your conscience? Come on, I know you have a heart in there somewhere." Mr J huffed and puffed, desperate to sway the adninja king.

"Mr J, you need to remember who is in charge here. I am. I have something you want, and you need to respect me more." King Brazi swooshed about as he shouted.

"You need to listen very carefully because I only intend to give you these instructions once." He waggled his wispy finger in Mr J's face.

"You will do as I say, and if it all goes smoothly, I can promise you will have your precious kakarooni back home. And I will be free from this zoo with cash in my pocket."

Mr J paused. He didn't answer straight away. He poised his wing on the tip of his chin. "Go ahead," he said finally.

"Your children need to complete the cheese board game. The kakarooni is locked in a cupboard at the end of the board. They need to deposit the money, and he will be released." Brazi spat in his face as he spoke.

Mr J wiped his face clean with his free wing. "So, where is the kidnapper, then?"

Brazi laughed that evil laugh once again. "I'm not going to tell you that." He laughed again and waited for Mr J's reaction.

"I thought you and the kidnapper were working together. What have you done with him?" Mr J asked. His body was loose, relaxed, and his face expressed no emotion.

"Never you mind! Now, enough with all the questions. Get on with your task. Go and fetch your tribe, and the game will commence."

"Very well, let's get this over with. Children, come here." Mr J beckoned them.

"Why do we have to go across the board? Why can't we simply give you the money, and you give us the kakarooni back?" Maddie asked Brazi as she and Theo stood by Mr J.

"Because the cupboard is locked. It will only open once the money is deposited. You cannot get to the cupboard without crossing the board. If you don't believe me, then look." He pointed to the cheese board.

He was right. Theo could see it in the distance. There was no way to reach the cupboard without crossing the board.

"Well, how did you get to the cupboard to lock up the kakarooni, then?" she asked, hands on hips.

"Like I am going to tell you that! Oh, and it isn't as straightforward as you might think. I've decided my lovely adninjas need a bit of fun. So, they will be following and hindering you every step of the way." Brazi screeched with delight. "If you can get across that board, defeating them in the process, you deserve your precious kakarooni. In fact, you can have the kidnapper thrown in as a bonus. He's a waste of space." Brazi laughed his head off.

• • •

The tribe was lined up and ready to play. Theo straddled across Croc's back and Maddie on Delphine's. Both pairs sat on the edge of the middle square with the giant grapes facing them. Mr J had explained to them what was happening. He gave them as much information as he could.

"You have one hour to get to the other side," Brazi shouted from his floaty position. He was hovering around the edge to their right. He could view it all from there.

It looked simple to the children at first glance. By now, both Theo and Maddie knew to expect anything in this world. They were as prepared as they could be.

"Here, take this. You will need it at the end." Mr J handed Croc a wad of cash.

The children were given helmets to wear while riding the animals. But the animals were not provided, so Theo and Maddie were grateful Croc and Delphine offered.

Mr J approached the children silently. "Okay, kids, quick tip," he whispered. "Try befriending the animals so they will let you cross through. I've heard the animals don't like people on their board. They'll do everything they can to stop you."

Once again, Theo wished he was confident like Maddie appeared to be.

Theo lifted his helmet, peeking out at what faced them. His palms were sweating. Mr J walked away to join the others at the sideline, ready to cheer them on. Brazi had given strict instructions that no one was to help. It was Maddie, Theo, and their chosen animals.

Maddie leaned over to Theo and gently squeezed his arm while flashing him a smile. He wished he didn't feel so nervous. Maddie was so super-confident.

"Theo, I believe in you. You are amazing. We can do this. Let's beat these silly adninjas now and get the poor kakarooni home." Maddie's voice was full of enthusiasm and encouragement.

The adninja king interrupted. "Right. Your time starts now. Off you go, you silly pair of children. See you when you are defeated. My guess would be you might make it to the middle!" Brazi laughed. "Go!" he shouted.

Off they went. Theo and Maddie planned to move diagonally to avoid all the goats and any other seemingly dangerous animals that presented themselves. Whether this would work was uncertain. But all they could do was move forward and hope for the best. They moved first from the grapes to the salami and meats. Each square was about the size of an average living room, but each had its own unique pieces.

Maddie and Delphine moved first. Maddie pushed the giant grapes aside and rode all the way to the back of the square, and Delphine jumped into the air as they crossed over to the salami and meat square. Theo followed suit. The goat in the corner of the square didn't bat an eyelid. He carried on munching away on cheese and grapes. He seemed happy enough. He looked them up and down but didn't seem in the slightest bit bothered by them. If it was going to be this easy all the way through, Theo thought, they had nothing to worry about. He felt his tension drop a little.

Croc sniffed the meat on the next square. "Oooh, can we have some salami while we are here? I love that stuff." As Mr J wasn't there to ask, none of them thought to say no, so they let Croc have a nibble on the meats.

"Yes, they do look lovely," Theo agreed. "I am going to have some, too." He jumped off Croc's back.

Delphine protested, "We should keep moving, guys. We don't know what we are going to face. I would rather be ahead of time. Come on."

Theo looked at Delphine. "Yeah, you are right. Sorry. Let's get on." He was about to jump back onto Croc when he slipped. He stepped in some Serrano ham and lost his footing. Maddie leapt off Delphine's back and ran over to help him up. She grabbed his hand, but as she pulled, he was stronger, and she fell on top of him. She giggled as his face burned bright red.

"Come on, get up, you two," Delphine snapped at them. Maddie and Theo jumped up and mounted their animals.

"I reckon we head to the nuts and seeds next," Maddie said. "What do you think? I think we should try to head across and then up the board. I think Brazi was winding us up. This is easy." Maddie smiled with confidence, feeling a bit too full of herself. She seemed to have forgotten that they had no idea what they were going to be faced with at any given moment.

"Yes, that makes sense, Maddie. Since it is next door, I think we can hop over to that square, then move on up. But don't forget it might not be this easy all the way through. We have to stay prepared and not let our confidence take over," Delphine reminded her.

They hopped over to the nuts and seeds, which proved to be an easy task. It wasn't until they jumped from there to the sauces and dips square that they ran into problems.

• • •

"Maddie, look out!" Theo shouted. She turned to see what all the fuss was about, but she was too late. An adninja kicked her in the side, and she hurtled towards the dips.

As she spun through the air, Brazi shouted, "Alakazaroo!" He was waving a wand about, no doubt trying to cause as much mayhem as possible.

As Theo was about to jump down and help Maddie, he noticed an adninja floating towards him out of the corner of his eye. The kick to his head hurt like crazy, and the force made his head spin. The next thing he knew, he was flying through the air himself, heading straight for the dips.

Theo heard the king's laughter as the adninjas floated away, and he saw Mr J and Rabwarf noticed them, too. They tried to shout to the children to warn them, but they were too late. The adninjas swept upon the children by surprise and knocked them off their animals, straight into the gooey sauces. Within a few seconds, they were both neck-deep in the sauce pots. Theo was grateful they could both swim, but he also felt his heart pounding with panic. He knew they were now losing time as they tried to get out of this sticky mess.

They swam about for a few minutes before Delphine and Croc pulled them out of the sauces. Theo moaned about being all sticky. "How are we going to get clean and dry?" he asked, stamping his feet. He had never felt so annoyed.

"There is no time to worry about that. We must move on," Delphine told him.

"Yep, Delphine is right, Theo. It's only a bit of stickiness, and rescuing the kakarooni is more important," Maddie said. He nodded, but he wasn't happy.

They moved on. Time was getting away from them, and Croc was panicking a little. Almost half their time had run out. They were pretty much halfway through, and it hadn't been too tough. If this were all Brazi would throw at them, they could manage.

They decided to go to the Stilton cheese square at their right. Delphine suggested the move.

"I think if we head through the Stilton cheese and around the goats' cheese, then we haven't got to worry in case the goat turns on us," Delphine explained.

They all saw sense in this and agreed. So, on they rode through the Stilton cheese square and up to the giant breadsticks, silently passing the next goat. They decided against stopping again as they wanted to complete the task as soon as they could.

This goat, like the other guy, seemed occupied with his food and hardly cast a glance in their direction.

However, as they made their way through to the other side of the breadsticks and up into the ports and wines square, they suddenly heard hooves galloping behind them.

Theo turned around first. "Argh!" he screamed. The goat was fast approaching, and he didn't look like he was in the mood for cuddles and a chat. Very quickly, a fight resulted. The adninjas turned up again, too. The scene fell into madness.

The goat tried to ram them off the side of the board. Maddie and Theo clung onto to their animals for dear life. The adninjas grabbed wine and port bottles and smashed them all over the place, throwing them about.

Theo and Maddie ducked down as much as possible to avoid getting hit. Theo winced as a glass shard grazed his shoulder. Through the chaos, Maddie shouted to Delphine.

"Turn back around! Go back to the breadstick square." Delphine didn't question her but motioned for Croc and Theo to follow them as well.

"Grab the breadsticks to use as weapons, and we can fight them off," Maddie said as they hit the previous square.

However, the goat and the adninjas followed them. So, they had to fight them off one square further back, which now meant they were behind again. It didn't take them long to fight off the goat. Theo and Maddie each seized a breadstick and jabbed repeatedly. The breadsticks were soft enough, and they forced him back without hurting him. The adninjas were a different story. They would not easily give in.

No matter how hard they thrust their weapons, because the adninjas were wispy shadows, the breadsticks swept right through them.

Croc whispered to Theo. "We need to lure the adninjas into a corner. If you and Maddie do that, Delphine and I can gather some wine and port bottles while they are distracted. The adninjas have some weird allergy to it. I remember Mincha telling me. It stings them. Let's head back to the wine square. Tell Maddie." Theo leant over to Maddie and explained the plan.

Delphine took the lead from Maddie and followed Croc back to the wine square, the adninjas closing in at their heels.

When they reached the square, it was such a mess—wine and port spilt everywhere and empty glass bottles strewn all over the place. The adninjas were sure good at creating havoc.

"Come get me, you silly adninja," Maddie said as she and Theo jumped off Croc and Delphine and ran into the corner of the square. While the adninjas followed them, Croc and Delphine grabbed a few bottles at the ready.

In one swift movement Croc and Delphine lurched forward, throwing wine and port all over the adninjas. Maddie and Theo managed to swerve and avoid the splash. They grabbed their breadsticks and threw them as well. This waylaid the adninjas, giving the tribe a few minutes to escape.

"Quick, this way!" Delphine shouted as Maddie mounted the dolphorse and Theo jumped onto Croc.

"There is a secret passage. It is the only way to leave this square," Delphine explained as they rode towards it. "If I remember rightly, it takes us straight to the dark chocolate square."

They now only had ten minutes left. If they went the wrong way, they wouldn't get there.

Delphine had to be sure to choose the right way, or they were doomed. They were faced with two doorways. One would lead straight to the dark chocolate square, and she had no idea where the other went.

• • •

"It was the wrong doorway," Delphine sighed.

They had arrived on another goats' cheese square. To their left was a crusty bread square. Giant slices of chunky tiger loaf took up most of the space. Delphine was certain the passageway closed after them, so there was no hope of going back.

"Now what are we going to do?" Theo asked.

"That goat looks like he is about to attack," Maddie added.

"I don't know," Delphine said in a shaky voice. "I was sure this was the way. But we have taken the wrong passage."

A second later, the goat snorted and ran towards them. He was fast approaching, galloping. Theo trembled, and even Maddie looked a little tense.

"Jump on. I have a plan," Croc said. Theo mounted the crocozeb as Maddie jumped onto Delphine. Croc didn't have time to explain. There wasn't much time left.

Theo felt himself lurch forward as Croc bolted up to the block of goats' cheese. It was a few feet away from them. Croc leaped high into the air and nearly landed on top of the cheese, hanging on by his two front legs. They had barely caught the edge. But he was slipping fast. Theo was shaking, petrified for fear they would fall any minute. He didn't know what to do.

Maddie screamed, "Hold on tight, Croc. Theo, climb onto the cheese and pull Croc up. You can do it. Quick!" She covered her eyes with both hands but peered through her fingers. Theo gritted his teeth and sucked in his breath. He knew he had to man up.

He started to climb Croc, and he had almost reached the top of the cheese when one of Croc's legs fell. This jolted Theo back, but Croc held on for dear life with the other leg. Theo's heart reached his throat, but he knew he had to push the fear down and continue. He crawled up to the top of Croc's shoulders.

It's now or never, he thought.

He looked around himself for a minute and then sprung himself forward, landing on top of the block of cheese. Croc still held on with his one leg.

Theo saw Maddie release her breath and remove her hands from her eyes.

"Yippee!" she shouted, clapping her hands.

Theo grabbed hold of Croc and heaved him up by his shoulders onto the cheese. They both dropped onto their bums as Theo shouted, "Look out, Maddie!" She heard his warning and turned to come face to face with the goat.

The goat bit at Maddie's leg and an adninja rode him, goading him on.

"Get off me!" she shouted at him. She kicked at his head with such force that he toppled over.

This gave Delphine and Maddie a few seconds to run and leap at the cheese. It was all they needed. Delphine had the advantage of watching Croc the first time, so she calculated her jump and went for it, running at high speed.

"Faster, Delphine. Jump now!" Maddie screamed as loud as she could. Theo watched them leave the ground. It was like an aeroplane taking off. The sudden force pushed Maddie's hair back, and her face muscles tightened. Theo's tummy did a flip. He silently prayed they would make it.

CHAPTER 14

Game Over

Maddie fell off Delphine as they hit the top of the cheese block.

"Yes, we made it. Woohoo!" Maddie was delighted. Delphine collapsed in a heap.

"Well done, you pair," Croc said, smiling.

From up there, they could see the entire board. To their left was the crusty bread square, and then the dark chocolate square was next to that. Delphine was still sure that was the exit.

"What is the plan now, Croc?" she asked.

"Hmmm, I'm not sure." Croc replied.

"Well, it might sound crazy, and it might not work." Theo said quietly, looking down at his shoes, "But maybe we can use the crusty bread as stepping stones. It's quite high. I think we can leap across," he explained as he pointed to the bread.

"I guess we have nothing to lose and no other option, really," Delphine said in agreement.

"Yesssss Theo, wicked idea." Maddie said, high-fiving him.

They made it to the dark chocolate square with a minute to spare. It wasn't the easiest task, crossing the large bread pieces, but they seemed to have lost the adninjas, which helped. Most of them, Maddie assumed, were stung by the wine.

As they jumped to the dark chocolate square, Maddie ran over to her favourite, fruit and nut, and stole a piece. The mischievous look on her face made Theo giggle.

"You are always doing something naughty." He laughed again.

They both removed their helmets and looked around themselves. Maddie bubbled with excitement and happiness that they had made it across the board. It was dicey in places, but she thought they did pretty well, overall. Theo looked exhausted. His eyes seemed to have shrunk, and he was struggling to keep them open.

They all trotted off the square and left the board behind them. Brazi was waiting, floating to their right. He didn't look pleased. Maddie stuck her tongue out at him, but this time she didn't feel the need to say anything. Brazi simply stared as if he had no words left to say.

"We did it, Maddie. Now we can release the kakarooni. How do we do that?" Theo seemed pleased. Maddie smiled. It was nice to see him becoming braver. They had been through a lot together on this journey.

"I don't know." Maddie turned to the adninja king. "Brazi, how do we release the kakarooni? We have completed the cheese board. Now you must keep your end of the deal." As she shouted, she made a beeline for the cupboard.

"Not so fast, young Maddie. Where is the money? I told Mr J you need to deposit the money. Look, there is a safety box. The money needs to go in there, and then they will automatically be released," Brazi replied, floating towards them.

"What do you mean 'they'?" Maddie asked. "Is there more than one kakarooni?"

Brazi laughed. "Hahaha, surprise! I have the kidnapper in there, too. It's a real bargain. You get two for the price of one! Now, get my money! I'm not in a great mood."

Croc moved forward. "I have the money. Where does it go?"

Brazi pointed and spat, "In the box, fool."

Once the money was safely inside, they heard a click. Maddie, Theo, Croc, and Delphine stood back. Maddie prayed this would work. She didn't trust Brazi one bit. She felt Theo's anxiousness as he tightened his grip on her arm. For a moment everyone held their breath, and time seemed to stand still.

The door to the cupboard cracked open. The kidnapper ran out, followed by the kakarooni. He was sluggish and moved in slow motion. He didn't look good. He needed his cold environment as soon as possible or else he might not survive.

"Oh, look, Theo. The game is fading." Maddie pointed to the board, her mouth dropping open a little. Theo's eyes widened as the cheese board disappeared in front of them.

"Cool," Theo whispered.

Mr J sauntered over to the children. "Well done, you pair. You did such a great job. Now we must get out of here. The kakarooni needs his home."

Brazi was distracted. The kidnapper had charged over and started to yell at him.

Maddie wasn't ready to leave yet. "Just one minute," she said to Mr J and the others. She marched over to the kidnapper and Brazi. They were still raging at each other. Well, the kidnapper was doing most of the yelling; Brazi was laughing at him. The kidnapper couldn't believe Brazi locked him away, and now he had lost out on the money.

Maddie butted in. "Mr Kidnapper, I want to talk to you." Theo and Mr J were hot on her heels. They knew how Maddie got overexcited and charged into situations without thinking them through.

The kidnapper stopped midsentence. Maddie stared up at him and saw that Mr J was right. He did have a moustache like her teacher at school. She didn't think he was very big or scary, though. She tugged on his T-shirt. He didn't look like he had much patience.

"What do you want?" he barked. Maddie wasn't put off by his anger. She saw Theo and Mr J hovering, glad they didn't try to interfere.

"I want to know why you did all of this. What makes you so angry at everything?" she asked.

"You wouldn't understand. You are only a child. Life has been hard, and I need the money to get away from it all." His eyes were wistful, as if recalling a painful memory.

"But Mr Kidnapper, life is for having fun. You adults worry too much. You need to relax and enjoy yourself more." Maddie spoke with all the confidence of an eight-year-old. She wasn't about to be swayed by a frightened man.

"Life is not fun for me. Like I said, you are a child, so you won't understand. It might be fun for children because you don't have anything to worry about yet. You wait till you get older and discover it isn't all rosy. Now, go away and leave me alone. I need to finish talking to Brazi and get my money." He turned his attention back to the adninja king, his eyes now overcome with a fiery passion.

Maddie backed down. She sighed, but left him with one last sentence. "Well, at least think about this. Imagine a world where everyone learnt to be more loving, a world where people chose to have fun and not worry about things. Try it sometime, even if it's only for a day. Do what you want to do without being scared and see what happens."

She walked away with Theo and Mr J at each side.

"Mr J, where did you get all that money from?" she whispered.

"Well now, that would be telling." He tapped his nose and winked at her.

• • •

They landed at the secret Head Office by travelling through the secret passageways for almost the last time. The green men were pleased to see them after winning and rescuing the kakarooni.

The unicwhales took the kakarooni back to his home after saying their goodbyes to Maddie and Theo. Rabwarf, Paul, and Mr J all came to Head Office with them. Croc and Delphine also said their goodbyes and returned to their homes. "I am going to miss this world, Maddie," Theo said. "It's been such a great time. And you are so good at talking to people. You really showed that kidnapper."

"I know," she said as she wiped a tear from her cheek. "I feel sad, too. It's been so good. You are brill', Theo. We have had such an adventure." She reached over and hugged him tight.

"Well, children, we will be sad to see you go home. But the mission is complete, so now is the time for you to return to your lives. You must go to the flower gardens and exit through the yellow poppies. We can't thank you enough for your help here." As Green Wonky Eyes spoke, Maddie was sure she noticed a little tear in his eye.

He continued, "We would really love to help the kidnapper overcome his anger, but I guess we can't help everyone. At the very least we don't intend to punish him. We will let him go without another word. Be safe, kids. And keep having fun."

Maddie ran over to Green Wonky Eyes and gave him a massive squeeze. She had tears in her eyes. Theo gave him a high five.

"We loved it. Thank you. We hope we can come back one day," Maddie said, almost pleading.

"Who knows, Maddie?" Green Wonky Eyes shrugged his shoulders.

They said their thanks and goodbyes to the green men with many sniffles and bittersweet tears among all the members.

"Come on, children. Let's make a move. We need to get you home," Mr J said as he dragged them away, and for the final time they got to travel through the secret passage to the flower gardens.

They came to a tiny door, which wasn't there when they first arrived at Head Office, Maddie was sure of it. But it was there nonetheless, and Mr J directed them towards it. Just like Maddie's previous experience, this tunnel was colourful. It had many different coloured squares all around the sides—pinks, blues, greens, and yellows. The same arrows pointed down the sides. All they could see was the black hole at the very end, an eternity away.

It wasn't long before they fell out the bottom as before. However, this time they landed inside the watering can from which they started. They had been shrunk again.

"How are we going to get out?" Theo asked, turning to Mr J.

"Rabwarf knows. Don't ya, old fella?" Mr J said.

"Oh, yes. 'Tis easy, kids. Follow old Rabwarf." Rabwarf waved his hand and pushed them one by one towards the spout.

It was a bit of a mission because they had to launch themselves through the spout. Rabwarf went first, and when he reached the top, he pushed the sprinkled end out so they could leap through the hole. The children followed his lead and jumped through the spout, landing on the ground.

"How are we going to get back to our normal size?" Maddie asked Rabwarf when they were out safe and sound. It was nice to be back in the flower gardens. She loved the beauty there, even though the weather had changed that afternoon. The sky was overcast and threatened rain.

"I'm not sure that you are, if I'm honest. Hopefully, the transition will happen when you leave here, Rabwarf answered, ever the honest dwarf rabbit.

Maddie and Theo made their way over to the yellow poppies. It was a sad time, but they knew they couldn't stay here any longer. It was time to go back.

"Mr J, thank you so much for such a wonderful time here and for all your help. I am going to miss you all so much." Maddie hugged him and Rabwarf tightly, and tears streamed down her cheeks. She didn't want to go. But she knew they had to be making a move. Theo didn't show any emotions, but Maddie noticed a lump rising in his throat.

She turned and hugged Paul. It was a special moment between them. They understood each other, and they both had a place in each other's hearts.

"I will find your daughter, Paul, and tell her how much you love her." Paul embraced her tighter. She saw his eyes well up as one lone tear dropped onto his cheek. She reached up and wiped it away. He looked into her eyes.

"Thank you. Her name is Paula. She lives in the flats opposite the deserted railway station." He managed to speak between sobs. "I think you will be back soon enough. I am going to talk to Mr J about making these dream worlds into reality. We will need your help with that."

"Really, Paul?" Maddie asked.

"Yes, now go on. It is time for the real world," he said, spinning her around towards Mr J.

"Go on, be gone with you. I hate goodbyes," Mr J said. "We will meet again. But you must go back to your lives for now. Go and spread some good in the world, you pair of amazing children. And remember to always keep having fun!"

Rabwarf was not so forthcoming with his words of goodbye, but the way he hugged the children said it all. And with that, Mr J rubbed the yellow flower petals hard and pushed Maddie and Theo through the magic portal.

CHAPTER 15

The Epilogue

"Come on, Theo. Let's go to the shop. You promised your mother milk, as usual. Maybe for once we should try not to forget it." Maddie coaxed him to cross the road and skip along to the shop. She liked Theo's mum. She had been around for dinner quite a few times and took a real liking to her. His brother was a bit strange, but she could handle him.

"Oh, yeah. Mum gave me some extra cash today and said we could treat ourselves to some sweets," Theo replied. A large smile spread across his face.

When they were ready to pay, the guy behind the counter smiled at them. He was very handsome and looked like he loved life.

As he passed Maddie the change, his hand lingered on hers. His grubby fingers lightly pressed into her palm. She looked up at him as he spoke, noticing that caterpillar moustache.

"You were right, you know, young Maddie. Life is for having fun!"

Three months had passed since they left Imagination World. Theo settled back into his life and felt happier within himself. The bullying at school stopped because he learned to stand up for himself. He realised that if he didn't play the part of the victim, they couldn't play the part of the bully. But Maddie had itchy feet. She was dying to get to the dream worlds again, but she had no idea how to contact Mr J. That meant she had to accept life in the real world for now.

Maddie and Theo often met up about twice a week. Having readjusted to normal life, they were both happy and spent a lot of time together.

Maddie started to teach Theo some Spanish. He was doing pretty well. In return, he gave her lessons on the guitar.

They tried a few times to return to the deserted railway, but it was nowhere to be seen. It was as if it had never even existed. But they were good at accepting things these days. Even Theo changed his mind and saw it as magic.

On this particular day, they trundled past the deserted area on their way back from the shop. Theo pointed across the road. "Maddie, look. There is a new yellow poppy!"

ACKNOWLEDGEMENTS

All my thanks to AAE for supporting me and helping me bring this book to print, especially Kary Oberbrunner. He and his team are fab.

To my editor and illustrator, thank you so much for your hard work.

To Lee Weeks (a traditionally published thriller author), who ran a writing retreat with my good friend Mandy Spray. After going on this retreat and learning a lot from Lee, I went away and wrote my first draft within three months. I am eternally grateful for my one-on-one sessions with Lee, who encouraged me to write a whole series, not just one book. She is an inspiration.

Mandy is a lifelong friend who has unconditionally encouraged me and offered lots of support with my writing.

To my good friend Maria Wood—who helped me find my deep writing voice and encouraged me to develop my writing skills through an online programme with Jules Swales.

Lastly to Bec and Deb—their ongoing love and support does not go unnoticed. Many times we went on walks and talked about Maddie and Theo and their adventures and whether this or that would work. And, of course, their professional help and knowledge with all my behind-the-scenes technical stuff—websites, mailing list, etc.—has been invaluable.

I could not have done this book without any of these people, and there are probably others. So, a huge thank you to everyone who has helped and supported me in some way.

ABOUT THE AUTHOR

Lucy has always had a passion for writing. Through her writing and love for creativity, she now helps others follow their dreams and passions, creating a life they love. She holds writing retreats, coaches people one on one and also runs abstract art workshops.

For many years, she spent her life being afraid to be herself. Always worried about what other people thought of her, she doubted herself and struggled to put her trust in following her dreams of writing and painting, two things that flow naturally to Lucy.

Today, she takes on a project with love, joy and all the passion she has in her heart.

Being a children's author lights Lucy up from the inside. She loves to tell a good story, and the freedom she expresses so beautifully across the page gives us an insight into the fun she has creating these stories and characters. They come to life through Lucy's colourful imagination.

Lucy now lives a life of flexibility and variety. She spends her days doing the things she loves, that make her heart sing. She lives in a raw, beautiful part of the country, by the sea in North Devon.

"From the early age of 14, I wanted to become an author. I've always loved being creative and have been passionate about writing since my school days. It's amazing that my dream has finally come true. Most importantly, I now have a lot more fun in my life and I want to help others create more fun, too—it is like being a child again."

END NOTES

To find out more about what Lucy is up to and how you can learn to have more fun, please visit her website:

www.writingfromwisdom.co.uk

Lucy manages writing workshops and fun writing retreats, offers personal mentoring, and also gets up to various other activities. She is part of a team with her auntie and sister. Together they run mental health workshops and retreats, helping people who suffer with anxiety, depression, and many other mental health issues.

Please visit her website to see how you can join in more fun with her.

She has also written another book—*The Table with No Edge*. This can be purchased through Amazon. You can join her mailing list to receive regular updates about her upcoming books. All information can be found on the website.

Printed in Great Britain
by Amazon